HER DESERT DOCTOR

MARIE TUHART

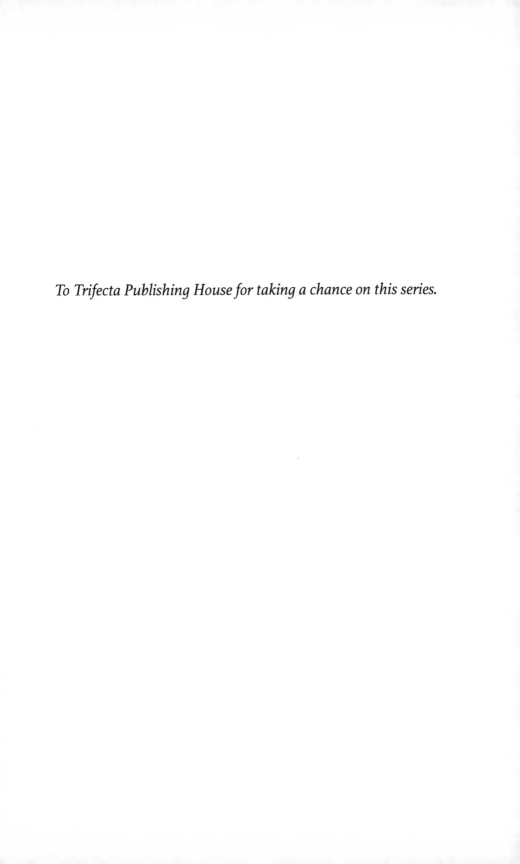

To Trifecta Publishing House for taking a chance on this series.

DEAR READER

The country of Bashir is a fictional place. They have their own customs and rules for titles. The title of Lady before someone's name is a sign of respect and not an official title.

In book one, once Catherine is engaged to Malik, she becomes the Crown Princess. Once they marry she will become queen.

In all the books, once the heroine is engaged to the hero they will become princess-to-be, and when they marry they will carry the princess title.

Published in the United States of America First Printing: 2018

Print

ISBN -13: 978-1-943407-53-8

E-Book

ISBN -13: 978-1-943407-54-5

Trifecta Publishing House

1120 East 6th Street

Port Angeles, Washington

98362

TRIFECTA PUBLISHING HOUSE

Contact Information: Info@TrifectaPublishingHouse.com

Editor: Elizabeth Jewell

Cover Art by Designed by Diana

Formatted by Monica Corwin

❀ Created with Vellum

Sara Fairchild pushed her blonde hair behind her ear before she walked through the double doors from the customs area of the airport in the small Middle Eastern country of Bashir. She was tired from not sleeping the last few nights, but energized to see her best friend. Customs was easy, but then, it did help to have the future queen's ear. A smile crept over Sara's lips.

Catherine, her best friend, was engaged to the new king, Malik. At times Sara had trouble believing it, but her friend had found true love, and she was thrilled for Catherine. Sara glanced around the waiting area. Catherine had told her there would be a driver to escort her to the palace.

Sara spied a man in black slacks and a white shirt holding a sign with her name on it. She strode over to him, admiring how his clothing molded to his fit and trim body. Her gaze continued to take him in ... dark hair, and ... her heart thumped. He had the most striking blue eyes.

"I'm Sara Fairchild." She stopped in front of him. His skin was tanned, and he was a couple inches taller than her five foot seven inches.

"Ms. Fairchild, I am Hassan." His deep, strong voice sent shivers of awareness up her spine.

Her mouth went dry. His voice reminded her of ... she shook her head. She was here to relax and to help Catherine prepare for her wedding. Well, the wedding wasn't for a few months yet, but Sara could lend Catherine moral support. And after she'd blown up at one of the lead doctors at the hospital, and thankfully her supervisor had agreed with her, Sara had taken a leave of absence.

"Let me take your bags." He took the handle from her hand and then glanced around. "Is this all?" He gestured to the bag he held and the carry-on over her shoulder.

"Yes. I travel light." She'd sublet her flat. Her heavy woolen sweaters and rainproof boots weren't suitable for Bashir's dry heat. Heck, most of her clothes weren't suitable for Bashir, and Catherine had told her the marketplace had everything she needed. So she'd packed a couple of pairs of jeans, some tops, lingerie, workout clothes, and running shoes.

"You do." He shook his head. "If you will come with me, our car is waiting just outside the main doors."

Sara followed him, admiring his stellar ass all the way to the main terminal. A gasp left her lips. The airport was beautifully designed. High ceilings with glass to let the light in, but even with the sun beating down it wasn't hot. She assumed the paintings on the walls were of local plants, animals, and people. A fitting welcome to the country.

They walked though a set of double doors, and the heat hit Sara. She stopped to get her bearings, and then continued to follow her escort. London had been cold and rainy when she'd left. Being somewhere sunny and warm was nice.

Her guide stopped next to a large black vehicle. He put her bag in the open trunk and held his hand out for her carry-on.

She gripped the strap. "I'll keep this with me." It held her computer and other electronics.

He nodded, shut the trunk, then opened the back door for her to get in.

Sara slipped into the cool interior of the car, surprised to see a man behind the wheel. Sara slid across the seat and placed her carry-on on the floor by her feet as Hassan climbed in and closed the door.

"We're ready, Najah."

Another shiver slipped through her body at the sound of his voice. What was it about the tone of his words? She couldn't stop herself from reacting to the husky, dominant voice.

The car pulled into traffic and Sara glanced out the

window. The desert lay off in the distance along with the city skyline before the road angled in a different direction.

"I understand you're here to help Catherine," Hassan said.

"Yes." She faced her guide and was surprised to see his gorgeous eyes trained on her. The bright blueness of his eyes and his wavy dark hair made his features seem more tan. "I'm excited for Catherine, but I know I'm here for moral support more than anything."

"Crown Princess Catherine has talked about your arrival."

"Oh." Who was Hassan to the royal family? Maybe a bodyguard. Catherine had mentioned, in passing, needing bodyguards. The sun reflecting off a building caught her attention, and she glanced out the window.

A large white building gleamed in the sun, and the red cross on the front was barely visible. "The hospital?" Catherine had mentioned the state-of-the art facility.

"Yes." He paused. "You sound surprised."

"Yes, no ... Sorry." She faced him and her fingers tangled together in her lap. "Catherine told me about the medical facilities here. I wasn't expecting something that impressive." And the building was impressive. From her brief view, she guessed it was at least twenty floors with several wings.

Hassan frowned at her. "You believe we are a third-world country?"

"No." The word burst from her lips. "I didn't mean that."

She shook her head. "I'm making a mess of this. I think it's wonderful you have a large medical facility."

"It is a first-class facility." His frown disappeared. "We're expanding our clinics out to more villages."

"That's wonderful. How are you managing staffing?" Excitement filled her. How fun it would be to be on the ground floor helping and teaching. *Remember, you're not here to work.* She shushed the voice in her head.

Her mobile phone rang, and Hassan shook his head. "Sorry." She dug it out of her purse and looked at it. "Excuse me. Hey, Catherine." He stiffened and Sara wondered why. "Yeah, I'm here and the flight was fine."

"I'm so excited you're here." Catherine's voice was bubbly.

"I am, too."

"So where are you?" Catherine asked.

"In the car with ... " The phone was lifted from her hand. She glared at Hassan as he placed her phone up to his ear. The nerve.

"Crown Princess, I am with Sara, and we're almost to the palace. We should arrive in about ten minutes." He handed the phone back to her.

"I'm back." Sara gave Hassan another glaring look, but he just grinned, totally unaffected.

"You're with Hassan?" Disbelief tinged Catherine's voice.

"Is there a problem?" She frowned. Had she done something she shouldn't have? Was she breaking a rule about getting into a car with a man she didn't know?

"No ... I'm ... Never mind. I'll see you soon, and I'll have tea and snacks waiting for you."

The line went dead. Sara frowned and put her phone away. When her head rose, Hassan was watching her. Sara swallowed.

Those piercing blue eyes sent chills through her body as if he could see all the way to her soul and know all her secrets. Sara cleared her throat. "Tell me more about Bashir, please?"

"I assumed Catherine had told you all about it." His eyebrows rose.

"A bit, but we mainly talked girl stuff."

"Girl stuff?"

"About the wedding and her life. Girl stuff." She wasn't about to tell him about their conversations around sex and kink. Sara was happy Catherine had found someone who enjoyed the same things she did.

Sara was a little more into the kink community than Catherine—correction, Sara had been. It had been too long since she'd been with a Dom, or had sex, for that matter.

"Bashir is a small country. We have been working at building up our economy and jobs for our people."

"That's wonderful." Sara smiled.

"It is, but it takes time." He shrugged and went silent.

Sara wrinkled her nose. Trying to pry information out of Hassan was like trying to move a boulder. "I was so happy when Catherine accepted the job to paint the mural at the hospital. Her work is fantastic." Maybe if she kept the topic neutral he'd talk more.

If she hadn't been staring at him, she would have missed the way his blue eyes softened. "The children love the mural. The Crown Princess is a miracle worker."

"Catherine has a way about her. She told me the children's wing was fairly new. Are there other new wings at the hospital?"

"We're about ready to open a drug rehabilitation wing. The hospital itself is only eight years old. Our previous ruler, King Jamal, had it commissioned when his son became a doctor."

Sara nodded. "That was a wonderful thing for the king to do."

"Our country needed it. Our people have health issues, and it makes more sense to treat them than ignore them."

"Health issues?"

"Getting our older population to understand the need to see a doctor is a struggle." He gestured with his hand toward the window. The town buildings were a mixture of new and old. "Some of our people don't understand why we need to embrace modern technology. They don't understand if we don't we will not survive."

"Difficult situation. Are you doing more public education?" She'd done some public education in England and, while this could be different, her palms tingled. She enjoyed helping people, all people. Her stomach clenched when she thought about one person she'd tried to help and couldn't. No, she had to put him out of her mind. It wasn't her fault, and it had been years ago.

"Working on it. As you can imagine, getting more doctors and nurses here is a bit difficult. Not many want to come here to live."

Sara frowned. "Why not?"

He let out a laugh. "Most don't want to give up the big city for our small country. We don't have a lot of nightlife. There are two movie theaters, and while we're not a dry country, there are not a lot of pubs or clubs."

"Dry country?" She hadn't heard that term.

"Alcohol. We allow it, but some of our neighboring countries do not."

"Ah." She let out a sigh. "I take it your younger generation doesn't want to stay and work in Bashir?" Suddenly she felt old. She was only twenty-eight, but she rarely went out, or partied, for that matter. She'd spent all her time on her career and look where that had gotten her. Nowhere.

"You are much too young to call them the younger generation."

"You're sweet to say so." She smiled. "I'm twenty-eight, but I'll admit there are days I feel a lot older." Especially when the doubts crept into her mind, like now, reminding her if she didn't watch herself she'd turn back into a scared nineteen-year-old.

"Interesting."

"What?"

"For someone so young to be so ... I can't think of the right word."

"I'm not that young. A lot of women my age are married with children already."

"But you are not."

"No." She shook her head and grinned. "I received my BSN at twenty-three, and since then I've been working my way up the chain. Two years ago I started taking classes so I could get into administration."

He drew back and his eyes widened. "Ah, why administration? Did you think nursing is not ... what is the word I want ... a worthy profession?"

"It's more than worthy." Sara's temper flared. Why did people always want to accuse her of abandoning her nursing duties in favor of administration?

"Then why the change?" He sat back and crossed his arms over his chest.

"Because administration needs to be more than just about the bottom line." She blew out a breath. "Who better than a nurse who knows about staffing levels, where the money needs to be spent, how budgets work, what doctors and nurses need on their floors for healthy patients? It shouldn't be about how much money is spent, but what to spend the money on." Sara closed her eyes and then reopened them.

"Your passion is admirable." A grin played around his lips, and she wondered what he was thinking.

"Sorry, I didn't mean to lecture you. It's just so many people think I don't like being a nurse. I do. I only want to do more."

Hassan al-Hakim couldn't help but admire Sara. She was a little spitfire when you got her going. It also proved to him that sometimes first impressions were wrong. When he'd first seen her standing in front of him at the airport, his first thought was that she appeared to be an ice-cold woman with blonde hair floating around her shoulders.

He couldn't believe this was Catherine's best friend. Not until she began to talk, especially about nursing. He'd discovered her passion; her fire and her green eyes were expressive.

A flash of arousal hit him hard and fast, but he fought it down. He hadn't had this type of reaction in a long time, and having it for Catherine's best friend wasn't a good idea.

But he loved her passion, her commitment to her work. He wondered why she was in Bashir. He knew she was here because Catherine wanted her in the wedding, but the wedding wasn't for a couple of months yet.

So what was the lovely Sara hiding? He would be happy to tease that secret out of her in the most delicious ways. A grin lifted his lips.

"Why are you smiling?" she asked, crossing her arms over her chest.

"You're passionate about your job." Would she be that passionate in bed? His libido jumped at the thought of having her spread out beneath him in his bed. Better yet, across his spanking horse.

He reined in his thoughts. He'd just met the woman. Let's not put the oxen before the cart. They didn't know each other yet. And he wouldn't rush into anything, not if he wanted it to be good for both of them.

"Some people don't understand there's more to the medical field than making money," she said, her voice soft.

"I do," he said quietly. He was pleased she saw the value in listening to the staff and their needs and not being focused on the money aspect. It was going to cost money to get the village clinics up and running. Maybe if he had her on his team, some of the pencil-pushing administrators would get off his back.

"That's great." She leaned forward. "Is that the palace?"

Hassan tore his gaze from her oval-shaped face. "Yes, we have arrived." He hadn't even noticed they'd left the main roadway.

"It's like a fairytale." Her eyes widened. Hassan looked at his family home.

The sun sparkled off the paint, and he could see how one might think of it as a fairytale. The palace had several floors and wings. More were being added, with Malik becoming king and his father stepping down. Both his parents wanted to slow down and have a more private life.

The car drove around the circular driveway and stopped. Hassan opened his door, got out, and then held his hand out for Sara.

A jolt of desire wrapped around him when their skin touched. He held still. Sara stood in front of him, her face turned up to his, her green gaze clashing with his. She inhaled and her tongue darted out to wet those rosy lips.

He wanted to ... no, needed to taste her. To feel those luscious lips against his. To see if there was a spark of attraction, of need. Hassan lowered his head. Sara's eyes widened but before his lips could touch hers—

"Sara, Hassan." Catherine's voice interrupted him.

What was he thinking? A groan escaped his lips. He straightened, but he didn't miss the disappointment that flashed in Sara's eyes. The kiss would have to wait. He turned and waved at Catherine, who stood at the top of the stairs.

"Catherine," Sara called out before darting around him and up the stairs.

He watched the two hug before reaching inside for her carry-on and then meeting Najah at the open trunk.

"You have a meeting at two, sir," Najah, his bodyguard, reminded him.

"Thank you." He glanced at his watch. It was already one. Hell, he wanted to hang around and spend time with Sara, but he couldn't. Taking her luggage, he climbed the stairs to where the pair waited.

"Thanks, Hassan." Catherine beamed at him. "Are you staying for lunch?"

"I wish I could, but I have a meeting." He set the luggage down, then turned to Sara. "Until later, my lady." He brushed his fingers over her pink cheek before turning and jogging back to the car.

Later he would explore with Sara, because something inside him had broken open at that near kiss. Maybe he should have made time to visit The Forum Club in London a couple of months ago. At least there he could let his dominant side out to play.

His dominant side was awake now and ready to play with Sara, and he didn't have a clue if she was interested or not. He would find out, but first things first. He had a meeting about the clinics to attend, and then he had patients to check on.

Sara watched the car pull away and gave a shaky laugh. What the hell had that near kiss been all about? It wasn't like her to kiss men she didn't know. But her lips still tingled, waiting for that kiss.

"Let's go inside," Catherine said.

"Sure." Sara reached for her bag when another man walked up.

"Samir, would you take Sara's luggage up to her room, please?"

"Of course, my lady." The man bowed and picked up her bags.

"Please be careful, my computer is in the top one," she said.

"I will take good care of it, my Lady Sara," Samir said and disappeared into the house.

"My lady?" Sara stepped into the cool interior of the palace and stopped short. The cathedral-style ceiling made the room seem massive. The walls were covered in paintings and maps. The wood floor gleamed as if recently polished. Off to her left was an ornate room filled with low sofas and chairs; Sara feared if she sat on them, it would ruin their luxurious features.

"Do you want to pick your jaw up off the floor?" Catherine said with a laugh. "I know; it's impressive. Come on." Catherine slipped her arm through Sara's. "Let's go into the family area." Catherine guided her through several hallways into a small room.

Sara grinned. This was more like it; comfortable-looking sofas and chairs were scattered around the room, and a colorful throw rug graced the highly polished floor. A set of large windows with the curtains pulled back allowed in natural light.

"So, the "my lady" title?" Sara asked again.

"Oh, that." Catherine waved her hand in the air. "Here it's a sign of respect and not really a title. Sit down." Catherine released Sara's arm and moved to the beige sofa. "Tea and scones will be here shortly."

"Only you would think of tea and scones." Sara's mood lightened. Catherine believed tea and scones solved all the world's problems. She sat down next to her best friend. "I'm so glad I'm here. I've missed you so much."

"Me too, talking on the phone doesn't quite fill the void like meeting in person." Catherine looked up, and Sara twisted in her seat to see who had walked into the room.

"Crown Princess," said a woman walking into the room with a tray. She set the tray on the table in front of the sofa, bowed, and left the room, closing the door behind her.

"Are you getting used to the pomp and circumstance yet?"

"Sort of." She waved her hand at the door. "That was minor. I've been told it will get worse once Malik and I are married." Catherine poured the tea, added milk, and handed it to Sara before getting her own cup. "So, tell me, how is it Hassan picked you up from the airport?"

"He wasn't supposed to?" Sara took a sip of her tea before setting her cup down. "You told me someone would be waiting."

"That I did." Catherine watched her over the rim of her teacup. "I didn't know it was going to be him." Catherine's gaze slid away from Sara's, and she wondered if there was something going on she needed to know about. She was about to ask when Catherine said, "So, tell me, how did it feel telling Doctor Doom off?"

Sara laughed, remembering her recent days in London. "You should have seen his face."

"Was it worth it?"

"Yes, someone had to take that obnoxious ass down a peg. I'm glad it was me." Sara sat back and relaxed. This was what she needed, to be around her best friend.

Hassan swept into his room at six-thirty. He had enough time for a quick shower before dinner. It was a dinner he had promised his mother he would attend, and he wouldn't disappoint her.

His mother wasn't aware he'd picked Sara up from the airport. He'd done it because Malik had asked him to. Malik was protective of his soon-to-be wife. Hassan couldn't blame him after Catherine's life had been threatened several times. Not that Malik thought Catherine's best friend would be a threat, but he wanted someone from the family to be there and make sure nothing out of the ordinary was going on.

So Hassan had agreed. If Sara hadn't met his standards, he'd have given Malik his honest opinion of her. But from the moment she'd spoken, she'd intrigued him. A smile crept over his lips as he remembered how Malik hadn't told Catherine who he was at the airport when they'd originally met. Although Malik's and Catherine's meeting had been a complete accident, his meeting Sara wasn't.

While he and Sara might clash a bit, it would be an interesting conversation between the two of them once he explained who he was. Circumstances were circumstances. Hassan didn't regret what he'd done. He was duty-bound to figure out if Sara was a threat to his family, which now included Catherine. He shook his head. Hopefully, Malik had explained this all to Catherine, or there was going to be hell to pay.

Hassan rubbed the back of his neck. His board of directors was not happy with him. Why couldn't they understand he wanted the people of Bashir to have the best health care possible? And that meant having the right people to help.

Which brought his thoughts back to Sara. When she'd talked about her view that helping people was more about care than money, her passionate nature came through loud and clear. That was his position too; it was getting the money people to see it that was a challenge.

He dried off from his shower and moved to the closet. While tonight Sara would be their guest, it wouldn't be too formal. He pulled out a clean pair of slacks and a polo shirt, his standard wear. He wondered what Sara would be wearing.

Today her clothes had been practical for traveling: jeans,

blouse, and sensible shoes. Yet her clothing enhanced her figure. His fingers tingled with the desire to see what was beneath the fabric she wore. He was still amazed at how his dominant side had roared to life the second she'd stood in front of him. Hassan shook his head. He'd have to see how tonight went before making any plans. He finished dressing and then went downstairs to the family-only area.

No one was in the family room yet, so that was good. He appreciated how his parents had made their family home separate from the public side. It was nice to be able to let one's hair down and not be judged.

Hassan moved to the bar. How was Sara going to take his deception? Well, in his mind he hadn't really deceived her, he just hadn't told her the truth of who he was, and she hadn't asked.

He poured himself a glass of soda. He only drank alcohol on rare occasions. Some might find it odd that Bashir didn't outlaw alcohol, but the country held a mixture of religions, and his family intended Bashir to be a secular country where they welcomed all religious beliefs.

Besides, he'd studied the problem and found that because alcohol was allowed, it was rare to find anyone in his country abusing it. No, the abuse came from opium or opioid addiction. His stomach churned. It was an uphill battle on that. So much worse than alcohol, although others might not agree with him.

How did one get the older generation to understand

smoking opium wasn't good for them or their health? Let alone the younger generation, who had discovered synthetic drugs, far more dangerous than anything else.

And then there was Fatima. Hassan sighed. His beautiful, loving ex-fiancée had succumbed to addiction, and he cursed himself for not even noticing. Two years had passed since she'd died, and regret still punched him in the stomach.

The rustle of clothing pulled Hassan out of his musings to see his father walk into the room. "Evening, Father. How are you feeling?" Several months ago, his father had had a mild heart attack, which had led to his stepping down and Malik becoming king.

"I'm fine, my son." Jamal grinned at him. "You don't need to worry, I'm following my doctor's orders."

"Glad to hear it. What would you like to drink?"

"A whiskey, but since your mother would have a fit, club soda is fine."

Hassan laughed and poured his father a drink. "This is better for you."

"I keep telling myself that as I walk two miles a day."

His mother swept into the room. "You walk those miles because you want to see all your sons married and your future grandchildren grow up." She crossed the room and kissed Hassan on the cheek. "Thank you for being here, I want Sara to feel welcome."

"Your wish is your command," Hassan said.

His mother laughed. "Your charming ways don't work on

me, you rascal." She glanced at her husband. "You had to give me all boys, didn't you?"

Jamal laughed as Malik, Catherine, and Sara walked into the room.

Hassan's blood rushed south and he swayed. Sara was wearing some sort of dress. It was a beautiful pale green, draped over her body, lovingly outlining her curves. His dick took notice and he shifted.

"Malik, Catherine, Sara." His mother's excited voice carried across the room before she walked over to them. She hugged Catherine and Malik before turning to Sara. "Welcome to Bashir and our family, my dear." She kissed Sara on the cheek.

"Thank you ... ah, Your Majesty."

"We don't stand on ceremony at home. I'm Anna." She turned and waved her hand. "My husband, Jamal."

"I'm pleased to meet you, sir." Sara held out her hand to his father. His father raised his eyebrows.

"Jamal. Welcome to our home, and may I say I'm pleased to be surrounded by such beautiful women." He took Sara's hand and kissed the back of it.

Anna sighed as Jamal released Sara's hand, and his mother moved to his father's side. "He's another one who likes to flatter."

Hassan almost choked on his drink when his mother winked. Heat radiated through his chest. His mother was happier than she'd been in a long time. Having his father step down as king and Malik finding the right woman seemed to give his mother renewed energy.

Sara's gaze found him and he smiled. Setting his drink down, Hassan crossed the room and took her hand. His lips caressed her skin before he said, "Hello again."

Sara barely hid her surprise at seeing Hassan in the family room. She hadn't realized he would be here tonight. Catherine had mentioned tonight would be family only, but he must be an extended family member. She was about to ask him when two more men walked into the room.

She bit her lip to prevent a gasp from escaping her lips. Did Anna and Jamal breed gorgeous children as a hobby? All boys, too.

"That is Khalid and Rafi," Anna said.

"Well, hello there." Rafi crossed the room and plucked her hand from Hassan's. "Aren't you a surprise?" He grinned at Catherine. "Do you have more friends like her?"

"Don't mind him." Hassan took her hand from Rafi's. Heat flooded Sara's body Where Rafi's touch had been pleasant, Hassan's was like an electric current. Oh, this was so not good. Sara needed to keep her head about her.

"Rafi is the family flirt," Catherine said.

"Family." Sara glanced from Hassan, to Rafi, to Malik, and then to Jamal and Khalid. All the men had dark hair and dark eyes, except Hassan, whose eyes were deep blue. "Who are you?"

"Hassan." Catherine stepped forward, a frown marring her forehead. "You did introduce yourself when you picked Sara up from the airport, right?"

"I did." His blue gaze captured hers. The heat radiating from his deep blue eyes singed her skin. "But I didn't tell her I was a member of the royal family."

"Hassan!" The outrage in Anna's voice caused Sara to smile. His mother wasn't happy.

"It wasn't intentional." To her amazement, his cheeks turned dark.

While she might find it cute he was embarrassed by his mother's anger, she was dismayed to find out he'd lied to her. And more so that she was lusting after royalty.

"Don't be angry with Hassan." Malik stepped forward. "I asked him to meet Sara at the airport."

"Well, at least he was more circumspect than you were," Catherine said, patting Malik's arm.

Sara remembered then about Malik meeting Catherine at the airport and what had transpired. "Thank goodness he didn't kiss me," Sara said with a laugh.

"Doesn't mean I didn't want to," Hassan said, his voice soft, and his lips close to her ear.

A shiver ran up her spine at the thought of those full lips on hers. Would it be a soft kiss? Or a commanding one? Commanding, she decided. There was nothing soft about Hassan.

"Don't tell me I need to apologize for another one of my son's antics," Jamal said.

Sara lifted her head and forced herself to take a step away from Hassan. "No need. He was a perfect gentleman."

"Figures," Rafi muttered.

Khalid let out a laugh and strode over to her, pulling her away from Hassan. "Welcome to our crazy family, Sara."

"Thank you." She glanced over her shoulder at Hassan as Khaild led her over to the bar.

"Drink?"

"No, thank you." Her gaze took in the people in the room. She'd been an only child, and while Catherine was her best friend, they were both kind of loners. During Sara's college days, she'd been too busy making sure to keep her nose clean to mingle too much with the other students outside of her studies. Then, as a nurse, she worked crazy hours, which didn't always match up with joining people at the pub or going to a show. In her opinion, she hadn't really missed anything.

She turned her gaze back to Hassan, who had moved to her side. "Your eye color is different," she blurted out.

Hassan laughed as his eyes lit up with humor. "Yes. I've been told I'm a throwback to my ancestor, who had blue eyes. Remind me to take you to the picture gallery and you'll see from the portraits there, people are correct."

Sara tilted her head and studied Hassan. There was something about him. Something that called to her. "That should be interesting."

"I think I need to clarify the family a bit," Catherine started. "Khalid is in charge of security, Rafi is in charge of the horses, and Hassan is a doctor."

"Which explains all the questions."

"What questions?" Catherine frowned. "Hassan, you did not interrogate my friend."

"Easy, Catherine," Sara said softly, placing a hand on her friend's arm. "He was doing what anyone concerned about his family would."

"That doesn't mean I'm happy about it." Catherine crossed her arms over her chest.

"Then be mad at me," Malik said, taking Catherine's hand in his and drawing her to his side. "I asked Hassan to pick Sara up and check her out."

"You what?" Catherine's anger flooded the room.

"It's okay." Sara hated that Catherine was upset. "You are a sweet, loyal, and true friend. But I understand. They are protecting you." She glanced from Catherine to Malik and then to Hassan. "He was a perfect gentleman and only ruffled my feathers a little bit."

"That sounds like my son," Anna said with a grin.

"That doesn't mean I have to like it," Catherine said, then huffed out a breath. "You and I are going to have a serious discussion." She patted her soon-to-be husband's cheek.

"Yes, my beautiful princess." He leaned drown and brushed a kiss over her lips.

Catherine sighed and broke into a smile. "Darn male." With her words the tension defused.

"And with that, dinner is ready. Shall we all go in?" Anna asked.

Hassan cupped Sara's elbow and followed his mother and father into the dining room.

"Are you mad at me?" he asked softly.

"No, but I would have liked it better if you were honest."

"Well, darn." She glanced up at him, surprised to see mischief in his eyes. "I was hoping I could get that first kiss."

"Maybe later, stud." The words slipped from her mouth before she could censor them, but no one seemed to hear but Hassan.

"I look forward to it."

Hassan led her to the chair next to him and Sara inhaled. His scent filled her. Pine, sandalwood, and pure masculinity. She'd have to watch herself. It wouldn't be proper to have her wicked way with Hassan at the dinner table.

Dinner was a lively affair. Everyone talked about their day, what was going on in the country, and life in general.

While Sara didn't contribute much, she was fascinated by the interaction.

"Hassan," Malik said as dessert was being served, "I received a call from Fazil today."

Hassan stiffened beside her. It was subtle. Without thought, she placed her hand over his where it rested on his leg. Over dinner, everyone had relaxed, including her.

"And what did Fazil say?"

"He wasn't happy about the request you sent in for the clinics."

"Malik, we've discussed this."

"Yes, we have. But he is the administrator of the hospital."

"He's a complete ass."

Sara was shocked at Hassan's tone and started to pull her hand away when his fingers captured hers.

"Look, I'm sorry, but without the money we're not able to expand and get the clinics up and running."

"I know," Malik sighed.

"I may be stepping out of line here, but what is the administrator's objection?" Sara asked.

"Fazil doesn't want the hospital to overrun its budget this year," Malik said.

"Is that a big issue?" She knew so little about Bashir's economy.

"Not in the long run," Malik said, sitting back in his chair. "We have oil exports in the west, the south is starting to run a profit in wheat and cotton, plus we grow a lot of our own fruit and vegetables. In the north we have the sheep and horses."

"Sounds like you have a prosperous country." Sara was impressed. "So why is the administrator protesting?"

"Fazil doesn't like that I want to open more clinics to help the outlying villages," Hassan said.

"Why? If the money is there, why not? Is it a personnel issue?" She glanced at Hassan before returning her gaze to Malik. He was studying her. "I'm sorry, maybe I'm overstepping my bounds."

"No." Malik waved his hands. "This is interesting. Catherine mentioned you were a nurse."

"Yes, I was." Sara swallowed. "I'm currently working on my PhD in administration."

"Interesting," Malik said.

"Hassan mentioned the new drug rehabilitation wing."

"Yes." Malik sighed. "Another reason Fazil is concerned."

"There's no reason. We have staff coming in to take care of the wing," Hassan said, his fingers tightening around hers.

"And you're spreading yourself too thin," Malik commented. "Hassan, you can't do it all."

Sara squeezed Hassan's fingers. "Have you thought about offering bonuses to anyone who is willing to come here and work for, let's say, two or three years under contract?"

"Now that's intriguing," Malik said.

"Force them to stay?" Khalid stared at her.

"No. Sometimes when there are nursing shortages, hospitals will pay a bonus to anyone willing to commit to a certain amount of time and work at the hospital."

"Does it work?" Anna asked.

"Most of the time, yes. I'm not going to say everyone is happy, but there can be a release clause written into the contract."

"Why haven't I thought of that?" Hassan shook his head.

"Because you've been too busy trying to do everything," Rafi commented. "Malik is right, brother. You can't do everything yourself."

Hassan sighed, but some of the tension left his body. Sara squeezed his fingers again.

"Sara, would you be willing to help us with this?" Malik asked.

"Now, son, that's unfair," Jamal interjected before Sara could speak.

"I agree," Anna said. "Sara is here to be with Catherine."

Sara's gaze met Catherine's. Catherine's blue eyes danced with mischief, and Sara bit back a groan. Her friend was plotting something.

"I think I can spare Sara a few days a week," Catherine said.

Hassan shook his head, and Sara's stomach dropped to her feet. She pulled her hand away from his in disappointment.

"I agree it's unfair to ask Sara when she's here to visit Catherine." Hassan waved his hands in the air.

"But," Sara started.

"No." Hassan's voice was hard.

Sara's temper flared. Yes, she was here to be with Catherine, but did Hassan think she couldn't help? Why was it men always thought women couldn't do the same job as them? Her appetite fled.

"Please excuse me." She pushed back her chair and laid her napkin next to her plate. "I'm no longer hungry. I'll be in my room." Without waiting, she stepped around the chair and strode out of the room.

Hassan stared at Sara's retreating back.

"That did not go well," Malik commented.

Hassan nodded in agreement, wondering what had upset Sara. He started to rise, but the look his mother gave him had him sinking back down onto his chair. She wasn't happy with her son.

"I'll go talk with her." Catherine stood and gave him a glare before she left the room.

Hassan glanced around the table and realized everyone was staring at him. "What did I do?" He didn't get it. Why was everyone mad at him?

His mother shook her head, and his father did too. Khalid drummed his fingers on the table. Malik grinned at him, and then Rafi laughed.

"Poor Hassan," Rafi said. "He doesn't even realize that he ordered Sara not to help."

"What?" Hassan shook his head. "I did not."

"Yes, you did, my son," Jamal said. "You said, very emphatically, no. No one in this room could mistake the tone behind it."

"But ... " Hassan cursed under his breath. Damn it, he hadn't meant it that way. He wanted Sara to be happy and spend time with her best friend.

"You blew it, brother," Malik said.

"Then it's up to me to make it right." Hassan stood. "Excuse me." He turned and left the room. But he didn't go straight up to Sara's room; instead, he went into the garden to gather his thoughts and figure out what he was going to say to her. Because he wasn't angry with her, only with himself for making a mess of things.

Sara wandered around the sitting room of her suite. She'd finally convinced Catherine to go back to dinner. Her friend was outraged on her behalf, but Sara had known this type of prejudice before. She just didn't expect it from Hassan. But why not? He might seem open-minded, but his forceful "no" had told her where she stood.

A headache pounded at her temples. Yes, she was here for Catherine, but that didn't mean she couldn't help. She almost had her PhD, and there was nothing wrong with her wanting to help, Catherine assured her. But she had to wonder if maybe she'd broken some rule.

It didn't help she was attracted to Hassan. Her attraction had no place in her life, not after Peter. Ever-loving Peter, who'd taken her love and plunged a knife through it. With a sigh, she picked up a book on the local history of Bashir Catherine had given her earlier and settled into the plush chair.

But she didn't open the book. Instead, her mind went over the last few days. Everything had been such a whirlwind from the time she'd told Dr. Doom off, to quitting her job, to packing, to flying to Bashir and having Hassan pick her up from the airport.

Her stomach fluttered. From the second she'd seen him, there'd been a pull, almost like a thread connecting them. It had grown stronger on the drive to the palace, and even before dinner it had been there.

Sara didn't believe in love at first sight. She couldn't deny there was an attraction between her and Hassan. But that didn't mean she had to act on it. There; that was settled in her mind.

She opened the book and started to read, but she hadn't even made it through one paragraph before a knock sounded at the doors leading to the balcony. With a frown, she set the book aside. Who the heck could be on the balcony? And knocking on her door? She was aware she was a woman alone, but the palace was guarded.

Sara pulled back the curtain. "What the heck are you doing?"

"Unlock the door." Hassan stood there, looking hand-some in the muted moonlight, his unique blue eyes serious.

"What do you want?" He motioned to the door. Really? He wanted her to unlock the door and let him in? Was he crazy?

"Come on, Sara. Let me in so we can talk."

"There's nothing to say." Hadn't he said enough at dinner? Feelings of inadequacy filled her.

"Open this door." His tone was low and hard, just like at dinner.

Her body responded to the command, and her hand reached for the lock before she came to her senses. "I'm about to go to bed," she lied. Damn, that was a habit she didn't want to fall back into. But it was a white lie, she reminded herself. And one told out of self-preservation.

"If you don't open this door, I'll break the glass, and everyone will come running."

"You wouldn't." Over dinner, Khalid had informed her of the security protocols. Guards patrolled the grounds and inside the palace as well.

"Want to make a bet?"

Stubborn, damn male. She unlocked the door and stepped back. He swept into the room and closed the door behind him.

"Why did you lock the door?" he asked.

"I always lock doors and windows." She crossed her arms over her chest and stared at him, wishing her heart would quit pounding at his closeness. "Besides, what are you doing here?"

"You only have to lock things when you're not here. There are guards. No one can get in without someone knowing about it."

"Just like Catherine couldn't get out without someone knowing about it?" She was fully aware her friend had slipped by security, twice.

Hassan chuckled, and his eyes softened. "I'll give Catherine credit, she was creative."

"And so others can slip in." The twinkle in his eyes caused her muscles to melt. Annoying reaction. "So what was so important you needed to come through the balcony door to speak with me tonight?"

"I think you misunderstood me at dinner."

"Oh." She stared at him, her temper flaring. "So you didn't lay down the 'lord of the manor' routine on me?"

"Yes ... No ... Oh, hell." Hassan ran a hand through his dark hair.

"Be honest."

"I am." He spread his arms wide. "What I said at dinner came out wrong."

"And what did you mean to say?"

"You're here to spend time with Catherine, correct?"

"Yes."

"I don't want to take you away from her." He touched the bare skin of her arm.

Shivers of awareness ran through her veins. She needed to get over the way his touch affected her. Otherwise, she would melt into a puddle at his feet. "Are you saying I can't do more than one thing while I'm here?"

"No." Frustration swept over his features.

Sara hid a smile and moved away from his tantalizing touch. She didn't want to get involved with Hassan. He was royalty, after all, and she was nothing.

"Sara." He took a step toward her. "I'm not doing this right."

"Just say it."

"I didn't mean to come off heavy-handed at dinner. I don't want you to feel obligated to help me or the hospital out while you're here."

"I don't." Was that what he thought? Had she misjudged him?

"Good. That's settled." He turned and went to the balcony doors. "Relax and enjoy your time with Catherine." And then he was gone.

The tension left Sara's body, leaving her lightheaded. What the hell was that all about? She shook her head, locked the balcony doors, and headed to her bedroom. What was she going to do about her attraction to Hassan? Nothing at the moment. She had to think this through before taking any action.

Samir held open the car door for Sara and Catherine. Over breakfast, they'd discussed what they wanted to do today and decided to go to the marketplace. Sara was excited.

"Crown Princess Catherine," a male voice called as flashes went off.

Catherine flinched, but it didn't bother Sara. After a short drive, she stepped out of the car with her head held high. Sara was proud when her friend did the same.

"I wish I was as poised as you are," Catherine murmured.

"You're doing fine." Sara squeezed her friend's arm. Together they walked toward the marketplace. "Try facing a group of yelling reporters wanting to know about the conditions of patients, and you can't reveal anything."

"I saw that on the news a few months ago. You never mentioned it."

Sara wrinkled her nose. "Dr. Doom was supposed to do it, but he was too stuck in his own head. I handled it because it was a part of my job to make sure people were informed— as much as they could be."

They turned the corner arm-in-arm with Samir following, and Sara let out a gasp. Stalls and people were everywhere. The smells of cooking meat, spices, and perfume collided.

"It's Sunday, there are a lot of people here today. Come on, I want you to get some more clothing since you didn't bring much." Catherine tugged her through the people.

"You're happier now, aren't you?" Sara asked.

"More than I thought I ever could be."

"I'm glad. Your life was so much different than mine." Sara's life had been relatively quiet, plus her parents supported her, no matter what she did or how much she screwed up her life. She'd been lucky. Catherine, not so much.

"It has been, but you're here now, and I refuse to dwell on the past." Catherine pulled her into the doorway of a shop.

"Crown Princess," a woman said with a bow. Her dark hair was pulled back with a simple black tie, and the caftan she wore was the colors of the rainbow.

"Oh, how beautiful," Sara said.

The woman smiled.

"Ramala." Catherine leaned down and kissed the small woman's cheek. "You know you don't have to bow."

"You are our future queen, respect is deemed."

Catherine looked at Sara and rolled her eyes. "This is my friend, Sara. She's going to be visiting for a while, and she needed some clothing more suited for Bashir than what she owns."

Ramala's gaze swept over Sara. "You young women, skinny things."

"Really?" Sara glanced down at her t-shirt and jeans. She certainly didn't think she was skinny.

Ramala waved her hand. "Always worried about their figures. A man likes to hold on to his woman." She slapped her hips.

Catherine laughed. "Well, that might be true, but you know how the press is unforgiving if I gain an ounce," Catherine said.

Sara frowned. She hadn't thought about that. "Catherine," she started.

Catherine waved her hand. "It's okay, I'm learning to deal. Besides, Malik reminds me every night that I'm his." A sparkle lit up her eyes.

"I bet he does." Sara laughed.

"Our king knows how to take care of his woman. Let's see what we can find for Lady Sara." Ramala turned and walked to the back of her shop.

The women followed, and Sara was amazed to see a sitting area, with low sofas and tables. Racks upon racks of clothing were spread around the room.

Ramala faced them once again. "Please sit, Crown Princess, while I figure out what Lady Sara needs."

Catherine sat down on the low sofa while Ramala circled Sara. A young girl walked in with a tray, with a teapot, cups, and some food. "Thank you. Please watch the shop while I take care of our guests," Ramala told the young girl before she scampered out of the room.

Sara fought not to fidget as Ramala walked around her. "I really don't need much," she said.

"I have ideas." She waved her hand toward a curtain-covered doorway. "Go disrobe, while I find what I want." Ramala walked over to the first rack.

Sara looked at Catherine, who snickered and made a shooing motion with her hand. Sara let out a sigh and slipped behind the curtains. She'd just stripped down to her underwear when Ramala strode in, arms full.

"Let's start with these and go from there."

"All of these?" Sara couldn't help but ask. There had to be at least twenty outfits.

"Yes, Lady Sara."

Sara shook her head, but took the first outfit and tried it on.

Three hours later, Sara was wearing a pair of tan slacks with a white blouse. And had more clothing than she needed for a year. Samir led them to one of the small cafes before taking her purchases to the car.

The cafe owner shooed off the press before seating them at a small outside table in the back away from prying eyes.

"I will bring tea and my very best pastries for you both." The owner bustled off.

"Is it like this all the time?" Sara asked. She'd noticed how the people greeted Catherine as they walked through the marketplace, many coming out of their shops. But it was more than that; many greeted her as well.

"Yes. The people of Bashir are friendly and enjoy having those connected with royalty visit."

"I'm not royal, but you are."

"Not yet." Catherine smiled as the man returned with tea, cups, plates, and a platter filled with pastries and fruit. "Thank you so much, Yusef. You make the best loukoumades."

"Thank you, Princess." He set everything on the table, bowed, and then left.

"He just called you Princess." Sara looked over the platter. So many choices, including melon, mango, and strawberries.

"Yes, when I became engaged to Malik, Jamal declared I was the crown princess."

"So you have a title." Sara digested the information. Catherine was handling all this royal stuff well. "This all looks delicious." Sara gestured to the platter.

"It is. I'll need to do an extra session in the gym. But it's so yummy." Catherine poured them both some tea. "The round balls are loukoumades. You can put honey or powered sugar over them. The triangles are fried almond pastries, the open triangles are baklava made with chopped nuts and drizzled with syrup, and the last is kahk, a cookie that is to die for."

"I don't know what to try first." Everything in front of her looked good. Sara picked up a cookie and took a bite. Her eyes closed as the butter taste burst on her tongue, followed by cream. "Oh, my goodness."

"Told you. Try the loukoumades. Yusef makes them fresh every morning."

Sara took two of the small balls and added honey to one and powdered sugar to the other before she ate them. She let out a moan. "Hell, I'm going to need to run five miles to work off this food."

Catherine poured them both some more tea and sat back in her chair. "So tell me about you and Hassan."

Thank goodness Sara's mouth was empty, or she would have choked on her food. "Excuse me?" Sara took a sip of her tea.

"Come on." Catherine waved her hand in the air. "We've been friends for a long time and were flatmates."

"True, but I don't know what you're talking about." She wasn't sure what Catherine was getting at.

"Liar," Catherine said with a grin. "You two were striking sparks off of each other last night."

Sara shook her head. "Those sparks were in annoyance." At least that's what she was telling herself.

"Bull." Catherine filled her plate. "I've never seen Hassan look at a woman the way he looked at you last night."

"Really?" Sara winced as soon as the word left her mouth.

"Busted." Catherine laughed.

"Okay, he is a handsome man." It was more than looks. There was something about him that melted her insides. Heated her blood and made her want to kiss him silly. She reined in her thoughts.

"He is."

Sara glanced around the cafe and then back at Catherine. "How freely can we talk without being overheard?"

Catherine's eyes widened. "If we talk softly we should be fine. The press are confined outside."

"Hassan came to my room last night."

"He what?" Catherine's voice came out in a harsh whisper. "What did he do?"

"Nothing. He tried to apologize for what he said over dinner."

"Tried to? He should have, Hassan was out of line."

"He was protecting what he's passionate about." Sara had had time to sleep on the entire conversation with Hassan. She'd overreacted at dinner, and her attraction to him was natural; her nerves were raw from what had happened with Dr. Doom, but it was more than that. Hassan called to her on a sexual level she'd thought was dead and buried.

Catherine tilted her head and stared at her. "You're coming out of your deep freeze."

"What?"

"Come on, Sara. You went into a deep freeze after Peter. How long has it been since you went back to the club?"

Sara closed her eyes, then opened them. "Not since that night with Peter."

"And that was three years ago. You were a mess after Peter, and denying a part of yourself isn't helping."

"You know what happened that night."

"Yes." Catherine reached across the table and squeezed

Sara's hand where it sat next to her plate. "And I was there to help you recover. But here's the thing." She looked around the area. "You know Malik and I are into kink."

Sara's eyes widened. "You and Malik?" She and Catherine had discussed kink when they were roommates, and a little bit on the phone but Sara was still surprised.

"Yes. You know I've always been curious."

"I never would have guessed you and Malik." She shook her head.

"If you haven't already noticed, all the al-Hakim men are dominant."

"I did notice that. I just thought it was being part of the royal family."

"That's probably part of it." Catherine took a sip of her tea. "Mailk and I, well, we're not into heavy play. He ties me up, spanks me, and uses toys on me, but that's about as far as we go."

"But is Hassan into the lifestyle?" Sara's curiosity was piqued.

"I don't know for sure. But if he is, go for it. Even if he's not, go for it. Since yesterday, your sparkle is back, and I've missed seeing it."

Sara laughed as the weight on her shoulders lifted. She had missed her best friend. "I have to ask, do you play at the palace in your bedroom?" Catherine's confession made her curious.

"Yes." Catherine's cheeks turned pink. "Trust me, there's lots of room. Just try not to be too noisy."

"Oh, my God, tell me."

"One night I screamed. I guess I was really loud, because the next thing I know, the guards are pounding on the door."

"They didn't rush in, did they?" How embarrassing that would be.

"No. Malik makes sure the door is locked, and he handled it. But I had a hard time for a few days meeting the eyes of the guards. Since then I've been super careful."

"How are you doing with the whole bodyguard thing?" She waved her hand at Samir and another man sitting by the door.

"Actually, not too bad. At times it's hard, but Samir is a good guy. It's not easy falling in love with royalty, so be careful." Catherine touched Sara's hand. "Do you want to tell me more about why you decided to come and visit now? When I asked you a month ago you said you were too busy."

Sara wrinkled her nose. "Can't I visit my best friend?" She was trying to delay the inevitable.

"You can, but it isn't like you, so spill."

Sara shifted in her seat. "It was an impulsive decision."

"You're never impulsive."

Bloody hell, she had a feeling Catherine would see right through her. "I was getting flack from the doctors and nurses about going into administration, and I wanted to get away." Okay, that was part of the truth.

Catherine frowned. "Why do I suspect there is more?"

Sara sighed. She might as well tell Catherine. "There is." She ran her finger around the rim of her teacup. "I told you about Dr. Doom?"

"What else did that asshole do?"

Her lips turned up at Catherine's words. While Catherine had never met the doctor, they'd talked about him. "He hated the fact I knew more than he did, not about medicine, but about the patients."

"But that's your job."

"He told me my job was to make him look good."

"Arrogant jerk."

"Yep, and about the time he told me that, I was already at the end of my rope."

"What happened?"

"I lost my temper." Sara wasn't proud of what had happened.

"I've never seen you lose your temper, even when that idiot Peter made such a scene."

"Well, I'd had a trying week. I was at the end of a fourteen-days-straight schedule. The nurses weren't doing what they were supposed to, I had to check up on all of them."

"I get that."

"I also was having to write them up because they weren't doing their jobs."

"Oh, now, that couldn't have been fun."

"It wasn't. HR got involved because of that, and then the

nurses started rumors about me. I just ignored them, and then Dr. Doom decided I was a threat to him." She plunged on. "We had a patient, a young girl. She'd been at a nightclub and someone slipped drugs into her drink. She was brought into the Accident and Emergency."

"Is she okay?" Catherine squeezed Sara's hand.

"Yes, but Dr. Doom kept telling her it was her fault, that she needed to stop dressing like a tramp and going out with strange men." The anger still filled Sara's veins as it had that night.

"He blamed the victim?"

"Yes, and she was a victim. The poor girl started to cry, trying to explain, but he kept talking over her. When the labs arrived, I read them. The poor girl had been given a drug cocktail of Ativan, Valium, and opioids. It was a miracle she didn't overdose."

"Holy crap."

"I walked into the room, labs in hand, and Dr. Doom just glared at me. I handed him the report and went over to the young woman. I took her hand in mine and told her everything would be okay. I told her it wasn't her fault. She needed to watch her drinks when out and never allow anyone to hand her a drink, have the bartender pour it in front of her and keep it with her at all times."

"Sensible advice."

"It was. Dr. Doom glared at me the whole time because I basically contradicted everything he had just said. He wasn't happy and asked me to step outside so we could talk."

"That must have been a fun conversation."

"Sure it was." Sarcasm dripped from her tone. In retrospect, it had felt really good to finally let go on the ass of a doctor. "So we stepped outside, and he started to ream me about how it wasn't my place, blah, blah, blah. I lost it and basically told him it wasn't the young woman's fault. He was a bad doctor for telling her it was. If he'd waited for the lab results, he'd have seen the combination of drugs in her system. She was lucky not to be raped or worse. She needed counseling, not some ass of a doctor who doesn't understand the first thing about people."

Catherine place her hand over her mouth to stifle her laughter.

"It's okay to laugh. Because I didn't realize how loud my voice had gotten as I yelled at him. By the time I'd finished, all the nurses were gathered around the pair of us, along with my boss."

"Oh, shit."

"I pretty much figured my job was over."

"Was it?"

"Yes and no. My boss shooed everyone away, told Dr. Doom to take a break, and then went back into the room to talk to the young lady, who had heard everything and was crying." Sara's spirit broke all over again as she remembered seeing the young woman sobbing.

"The poor girl. None of it was her fault."

"No, it wasn't. Luckily my boss agreed with me. She called in another consultant, we were able to transfer the young girl to another facility, and last I heard she was doing quite well."

"I bet Dr. Doom wasn't happy."

"Understatement of the century. He brought me up on charges of insubordination."

"Damn, asshole."

"Yeah. My boss told me she would fight the charges, but I honestly didn't have it in me. I resigned on the spot, called you, and here I am."

"You let Dr. Doom get away with his charges?"

"Not exactly." Sara wasn't exactly proud of herself, but she wasn't sorry either. "I stopped by the hospital before I went to the airport to pick up my last paycheck and talk with my boss. Dr. Doom was in her office, ranting and raving not only about me but the other nurses. My last nerve snapped."

"What happened?" Catherine leaned forward.

"I kind of went nuclear on his ass. Told him if he listened to patients rather than thinking he was always right, then maybe he'd understand patients better. And his bedside manner needed an overhaul, along with his outdated thinking. Then I took my paycheck and told him to go to hell."

More laughter burst from Catherine. "Oh, my goodness, I wish I could have seen his face."

"Yeah, well, I figured I probably wouldn't be able to work

as a nurse or an administrator anywhere in England. Maybe anywhere."

"That's total bullshit, if it happens. You are a fantastic nurse and would make a great administrator. Besides the fact you were right."

"Thanks." Sara let out a breath. It actually made her feel better talking to her best friend.

"I have an idea." Catherine poured them more tea.

"Why does that make me nervous?"

"I'm being serious. Why don't you help Hassan with getting the clinics set up?"

"He doesn't like people like me," Sara said, recalling his words from dinner the previous night about the hospital administrator.

"What do you mean?"

"Administrators."

"Why would he think poorly of you? He doesn't like Fazil because he's always about the bottom line, not about what is good for the people. You, on the other hand, always think of the patient first."

"But I came here to spend time with you." Sara wasn't sure why she was protesting. Working with Hassan would give her the last of the experience she needed to finish her PhD.

"We'll still spend time together. We're going to take the Arabic classes together. While almost everyone speaks

English, I need to learn their native language. And it will help you when you help Hassan in the villages."

"Catherine, I don't know if this is a good idea." Yet excitement filled her veins at the thought of doing something good here in Bashir.

"It's perfect. Now, let's go over what I know, and then I'll set up a meeting with Malik, Khalid, and Hassan."

"Why Khalid?"

"Security. He's in charge of it, and there's no way you're not going to be protected while you're here."

Sara raised her eyebrows. "I thought Bashir was safe?"

"It is, but you're going out to the villages." Catherine waved her hand. "I'll have Malik explain. Let's finish our snack so I can call this meeting."

Sara didn't argue, knowing that trying to change Catherine's mind was futile.

3

Sara brushed her hands down her skirt, smoothing out nonexistent wrinkles. Catherine had had to wait until Tuesday night to arrange the meeting, but the last two days had been fun, at least for Sara.

The Arabic lessons on Monday and Tuesday were enjoyable, and Sara was already picking up the language. Catherine would just stick her tongue out at her each time she picked up a new word.

"Nervous?" Catherine asked.

"A bit. Are you sure this is a good idea?"

"Yes." Catherine knocked on the door before opening it.

Sara swallowed as Malik, Khalid, and Hassan looked at them. It wasn't like she hadn't seen them in the last few days;

she had. Mainly at dinner, but for some reason she was really nervous now.

"Come in, ladies, I'm curious why Catherine called this meeting," Khalid said.

Sara looked at her friend, who just smiled, took her by the arm, and guided her inside to a chair.

"I wanted to discuss the possibility of Sara helping Hassan with the clinics," Catherine said. "I know I brought it up at dinner the other night and was met by opposition." Her gaze turned to Hassan.

Sara saw his eyes darken, but he stayed relaxed, leaning against the wall and watching her. She swallowed and forced her gaze back to Catherine.

"But I think it's a good idea."

"Sara?" Malik asked.

"I would like to help." She waved her hand in the air. "There's only so much I can help Catherine with. And I would welcome the chance to learn more about Bashir along with helping the people. You don't even have to pay me."

Malik nodded, then turned to Khalid. "Security issues?"

"Nothing that can't be handled. I've already hired some new men from different countries with extensive training. They'll be here tomorrow," Khalid said.

"Hassan?"

Sara waited, not daring to breathe. One objection from him and this would all be for nothing. "I'd like to speak to Sara alone for a few minutes."

Her stomach cramped. Malik nodded, and the room was cleared except for her and Hassan. The closing of the door sounded loud to her ears.

"Are you going to object?" she asked quietly.

Hassan crossed over to her. He leaned against the desk and stared down at her. "Why do you want to help?"

Well, at least he wasn't shutting her down. "Because I think it's important." She waved her hand in the air. "You're trying to do some good, but your family is right—you can't do it alone. I'm here. I can help."

"You came to visit Catherine."

"Yes, but that doesn't mean I can't help. I'm used to being busy. Catherine has duties I can't help with." She squirmed under Hassan's steady stare.

"Do you realize that will mean we'll be spending a lot of time together?"

Sara nodded, as hope filled her.

Hassan straightened, reached down, and cupped Sara's elbow, bringing her to her feet and close to him. "I'm attracted to you."

Her heart pounded in her chest. She tried to move away from his tantalizing touch, but he tightened his hold on her. She couldn't afford to get involved with him. He was royalty.

"That doesn't mean you have to act on it."

Mischief filled his blue eyes. "Are you saying you're not attracted to me?"

"I didn't say that." She clamped a hand over her mouth.

How the hell could she have admitted that? Dang, the man tied her up in knots without trying.

His eyes twinkled. "So I'm not in this alone."

"I don't mix work and play." Sara scrambled to find her balance. This man could knock her off her game faster than a speed pitcher.

"I might have to change your mind about that." He tugged her yet closer.

"I would think sexual harassment laws are the same here as in any other country." Where the hell had that come from? She didn't think he was sexually harassing her.

"Whoa." Hassan lifted his hands, allowing her to take a step back from his hard body. "First off, I didn't mean it that way, and second, I won't be your boss since you are volunteering to help."

"I'm sorry." She was. "I was out of line."

"Yes." His hands framed her waist. "But that doesn't mean I'm going to back off."

"Hassan." She brought her hands up and rested them on his shoulders, and he tugged her closer.

"I'm not going to hurt you," he murmured, his lips a hair's breadth away from hers.

"I ..." she said, then his mouth covered hers.

Her brain went blank as his tongue traced her lips and she opened up to him. It was crazy. She was crazy. Yes, she was attracted to him. His dominant ways called to her in a way she hadn't felt in a long time.

His tongue teased hers, and she dueled with it, relaxing into his embrace. It had been too long since she'd been held, kissed. His hands skimmed from her waist to her face, holding her steady as he ravaged her mouth.

Part of her was aware she should be pushing him away, but instead, her arms curled around his neck, her fingers sinking into his dark silky hair as the kiss continued. She shifted on her feet. Her core tightened. Her clit throbbed with need.

Hassan broke the kiss and rested his forehead against hers. "You taste like a fine wine and sunshine."

"How does sunshine taste?"

"Fresh, clean, delicious." His breath fanned her face.

"This wasn't a good idea." Her brain was coming out of its sensual haze.

"It was perfect. And there will be more."

A knock on the door caused her to jump. "Did you kill Sara?" Malik's voice carried through the door.

"No." Hassan answered back. "We'll continue this later," he said softly to her, then he gently pushed her several steps back.

"There won't be a later." Sara shook her head and crossed the room. She couldn't be close to him, or she'd beg him to take her back into his arms. A sense of homecoming flooded her body.

"Yes, there will." He adjusted his slacks before saying, "It's safe to come in."

The door opened and Malik poked his head in. "So, what is the verdict?"

"Sara is more than welcome to help me with the clinics."

"Yes," Catherine yelled, and Sara winced.

She was stuck now. Hassan had agreed, and she couldn't back out without explaining why. She closed her eyes and promised herself that she would behave. No more kissing Hassan, but she had a feeling that promise would be broken rather quickly.

Hassan hid a grin. He'd thrown Sara off balance, and he liked it. She wasn't indifferent to him. Good.

"Meet me in the foyer at seven tomorrow morning." With that, he strode out of the room. He jogged up the stairs to his suite. After a quick change of clothes, he made his way to the home gym.

He climbed on the treadmill, set the controls, and started the machine. He couldn't go out jogging at night, so this was the next best thing to work off his frustrations. Maybe he should've taken a quick trip to The Forum in London when he'd had the chance a few months ago.

At least there he could work out his need for control. Sara wasn't going to let him control her, at least not professionally. He didn't care about that, but in the bedroom ... he'd control every aspect of their lovemaking.

Her green eyes had been glazed over with passion after they'd kissed, and he hadn't missed the little sounds of pleasure she'd made while they kissed. His dick swelled and he ran faster.

But something frightened her? Was it his dominance? He frowned. Tomorrow he'd be a strict professional and see what happened. But when they got back to the palace, the gloves were coming off. Sara aroused him like no other woman.

The treadmill began to power down. He glanced at the counter. He'd run three miles without even realizing it. He walked for another ten minutes until the machine stopped.

Hassan grabbed the towel he'd thrown on the chair and wiped the sweat off his face. Tomorrow was a new day, and he was going to take full advantage of it.

Hassan walked into the foyer the next morning, surprised to see Sara there waiting for him. "Good morning," he said with a smile.

"Good morning."

Her voice was cheery. He studied her face and saw the fine lines around her eyes and the slight smudges of darkness beneath them. "Not to be insensitive, but you look like you had a long night." It was bad enough he hadn't fallen asleep until early this morning, he hated to think she'd suffered as well.

She pushed her blonde hair away from her face and stared at him. "As a matter of fact, I did. But it's okay, I can make it through the day with enough caffeine." She held up a travel mug. "Shall we go?"

He let out a chuckle. Hassan wanted to insist she stay home and rest, but she'd just ignore him. "All right, but I want to know if you start feeling too tired. The car will be available to bring you back here."

"Thank you."

He opened the front door and gestured for her to precede him. Normally he would drive himself to the hospital, but today he chose to have them driven. Khalid was insistent that Sara have a bodyguard, so he'd volunteered his own.

"Morning, Najah," he said when they reached the vehicle. "This is Sara."

"Hello, Najah," Sara said.

Najah smiled, and Hassan was amazed she'd pronounced it right, but then he remembered she'd been taking lessons with Catherine.

"My Lady Sara, it is a pleasure to meet you." Najah bowed and then opened the door for them to get in.

Hassan glanced at Najah before he climbed into the car. While the title of "Lady" was a term of respect in his country, it was the way Najah had said it. The same way Samir had called Catherine "Lady Catherine," long before anything official. Najah climbed into the front, next to the driver, and off they went.

After they pulled through the palace gates, Hassan turned to Sara. "There are a few things I need to let you know."

"Okay."

"Najah will be your bodyguard, so where you go, he goes."

"Do I really need him around the hospital?"

"Yes."

"All right. What else?" She took a sip from her mug and let out a moan.

His body reacted to her moan. No matter how much he told his dick to stand down, it grew hard no matter what. He shifted in his seat. "If I came on too strong last night in Malik's office, I'm sorry."

Sara glanced out the window and then back at him. "You didn't," she said softly. "I'm just not ready for any type of relationship."

Her honesty made him happy. "You said you were attracted to me."

Her gaze skidded away from his. "Yes."

Elation filled his veins. "Are you willing to see where this attraction goes?"

"I'm not sure." She placed her travel mug in the cup holder and clasped her hands together. "I don't want people to think I'm using you."

Surprise hit him in the gut. He hadn't thought of that, but he also knew it wasn't true. "I can keep it professional on the job." She kept her gaze downcast, and Hassan's dominant side pushed forward. "Sara, look at me." He kept his voice low, but his tone was commanding. Her lashes rose, and her startled green eyes met his.

His mouth fell open. She'd obeyed. He almost shouted in joy. His fingers itched to touch her creamy cheek, but he held back. Later, he promised himself.

"Here's my promise to you," he started. "On the job, we are professionals. But outside the hospital or clinic walls anything goes. Can you agree with that?" He wouldn't demand a relationship from her, but he did want to explore this attraction and her possible submission.

She was silent, but she held his gaze. Had he pushed her too far too fast?

"I can deal with that."

His dominant side danced in celebration, while his professional side reminded him they would be at the hospital soon. "Good. Now, let me tell you about the hospital."

Sara couldn't believe she'd agreed with Hassan. But when he'd used his commanding voice, damn if her submissive side hadn't responded. Her body quivered with need, want, and downright desire.

Was he aware of kink? It was possible, based on what Catherine had told her about her relationship with Malik. Sara had discovered kink during her university years. It helped her control herself when she was stressed.

Hassan's deep voice drew her in and kept her enthralled while he spoke about the hospital, how it was staffed, and what he wanted to accomplish. She also heard his frustrations around the current administrator, Fazil.

The car turned, and she caught sight of the big white building. She leaned forward and stared out the window.

"What made you decide to build the hospital versus just having clinics?" While a hospital with good operating rooms was important, Bashir wasn't a huge country.

"Clinics were nice, but we couldn't take care of the more critical patients. We needed to ship them to nearby countries. It wasn't easy on the families when a child had to be sent to another country."

"Understandable." Catherine had told her about the children's wing. "But why not something on a smaller scale, more specialized." Not that she wasn't excited, but did she really have the right skills to help him with the clinics? Doubts crept into her mind.

"It wasn't originally intended to be so big, but once we started, we just kept adding on."

The car pulled to a halt, and Hassan opened the door and

stepped out. Sara slid across the seat. Hassan held his hand out to her, and she placed hers in it. A shiver of awareness slid over her skin.

Be professional, she reminded herself. She glanced at the entrance to the hospital. The windows gleamed in the metal frames. Hassan kept ahold of her hand and guided her inside.

"This is the main lobby."

Sara was impressed, as not only did the lobby hold chairs, sofas, and tables, but there was a large information desk and right next to it a sign that said 'volunteers'. The lobby itself was painted in a light beige, and the furniture was soothing and looked comfortable.

The tile floor beneath her feet gleamed, and the carpeted area was spotless. She wondered what they were paying the maintenance people to keep it so immaculate.

"Our first stop," Hassan said, "will be HR, so we can get you a badge."

"That would be nice. I'm anxious to get started."

The next few hours, Sara spent filling out paperwork, then getting her picture taken and a badge. She was impressed with how the HR department was run. When she was done, the HR person took her up to the fourth floor, to an office that held a desk, a chair, and a file cabinet.

"I'll let Doctor Hassan know you're here, if you'll wait here." The woman walked away.

Sara sighed. She opened the desk drawers to find them

empty. Well, she was going to need supplies. Sara was about to see if she could go find someone when a young woman popped her head inside the doorway.

"Hi, I'm Izza." Her smile made Sara instantly at ease.

"I'm Sara." She held out her hand to the bubbly woman. Izza was a few inches shorter than Sara. Her black hair was neatly coiled into a bun at the back of her head. Sara's own hair was already escaping and tickling her skin. "Did Hassan send you?" Izza wore a top with elephants all over it along with a pair of white pants.

"I'm so glad to meet you. And yes, Dr. Hassan sent me to help you settle in and to help you if you need anything." The young woman's dark eyes were wide.

"Dr. Hassan?"

"Dr. Hassan gets upset if we use his last name, he prefers us to use his first name," Izza said.

Interesting. Sara smiled. "All right. I could use some help. At the moment, I need some paper and a pen so I can start making a list."

"Be right back." Izza scooted off and then came careening back into the office a few minutes later. She held out a pad of yellow paper and a box of pens. "I wasn't sure what type of pen you wanted, so I brought different ones." The words came out in a rush.

"Thank you." Sara took the supplies from her. "Why don't you go grab a chair for yourself?"

"Sure."

While Izza went to find a chair, Sara sat down and looked at the pens in the box. After finding an extra fine point, she started making notes on the pad. She glanced up as Izza wheeled in a chair.

"Are you one of the nurses here?" Sara asked.

"Yes. I just graduated with my RN degree." Izza beamed at her, and Sara couldn't help but grin at Izza's enthusiasm.

"Is there a nursing school here in Bashir?" That would solve some of their employment issues.

"No, I wish there were. I hated leaving my family for my schooling."

Sara could understand that. "Where did you get your training?" She continued writing down the supplies she needed.

"In France. It was a wonderful learning experience, and since I took French here in Bashir, it was a perfect fit."

Just then an older woman came rushing into the room. "Izza, I need you to go back to the children's ward where you belong." The woman didn't even glance at Sara.

"Dr. Hassan said ... " Izza started.

"I don't care what he said. You don't have time to be talking to this woman, you have work to do."

Sara's hackles rose. "Excuse me. I'm Sara, and I'll be helping Dr. Hassan with setting up the clinics."

"Rahma, head nurse. You can go back to what you were doing." She waved a dismissing hand at Sara.

"Rahma, where is Dr. Hassan?" Sara kept her tone pleasant. She didn't want to antagonize the woman, but without help she wasn't going to get anything done today.

"In the children's ward. Come, Izza." Rahma turned on her heel and marched away.

Izza shook her head. "I'm sorry."

"Don't be. Let us both go to the children's ward. I would love to see Catherine's mural."

"You know the crown princess?" Izza asked, awe in her voice.

"She's my best friend." Sara took in the empty nurse's desk and the lack of computers on the children's floor when they walked through. Rahma was nowhere to be seen.

"The crown princess is so nice, she spends a lot of time in the children's ward. They love her."

"I bet." The news didn't surprise Sara. Catherine had told her all about her and Malik's plans to make a little boy named Zain, an orphan, their ward.

Izzy led her into the ward. Hassan was standing next to a bed talking to a little boy, examining his hands. Sara held back, not wanting to disturb him.

"You're doing really great, Zain," Hassan said in a soft voice. "I'm really proud of you, and I know Catherine will be when she comes to visit."

The boy nodded, and Sara glanced around the room. There were other children occupying the beds, many asleep. The mural on the wall captured her attention. Oh, yes, this was definitely Catherine's work. Elephants and giraffes, with lots of trees, even an oasis. Catherine was a miracle worker in making the scenes come to life around all the medical equipment mounted to the walls.

Sara shifted, and Zain's gaze slid to her. She smiled and gave him a wave. He smiled at her, and Hassan turned. Just then Rahma bustled in.

"Izza, go take care of those towels and stuff." Rahma waved her hand before glancing at Sara. "Why are you here?"

Hassan straightened and frowned. "Please excuse me, Zain. I need to take care of Miss Sara." Hassan ruffled the boy's dark hair before he stood and walked over to Sara, Izza, and Rahma.

"Sorry to bother you," Sara said.

"You should be." Rahma huffed out a breath. "Dr. Hassan is busy."

Hassan features tightened. He turned to Izza. "Would you make sure the children don't need anything?"

"Of course, Dr. Hassan." Izza scampered off.

He cupped Sara's elbow. "Nurse Rahma, out in the hall, please." Hassan guided Sara into the hallway and away from the door to the children's ward. He kept his arm around her when he stopped and waited for Rahma to catch up to them.

"Hassan—" Sara started.

He shook his head, but his closed features told her he was hanging on to his temper by a thread. She wanted to talk with him before he spoke to Rahma, but it wasn't going to happen.

"Dr. Hassan, there are a million and one things to do," Rahma said, stopping next to them.

"Why are you being so rude?" Hassan asked.

The woman's face flushed. "I can't afford to lose a nurse to show this woman around." She waved her hand at Sara.

Hassan tightened his arm around her waist. "Sara is here to help set up the clinics. But what about Izza? She is one of your nurses."

"Izza can be lazy."

Sara's mouth dropped open. While she didn't know Izza that well, so far the young woman seemed to want to help.

"Really?" He raised his eyebrows at Rahma, and his blue eyes went glacial.

"What is going on here?" A male voice caused Sara to turn her head.

An older man strode toward them. His dark hair was beginning to turn gray, his face was lined with stress, and he smelled of wildflowers.

"Fazil," Hassan said. "Sara, this is Fazil, he's our current hospital administrator."

"Sir, it's good to meet you," Sara said, holding out her hand.

Fazil looked at her hand and waved it away. "Hassan, what is going on? I just got notice that HR added a consultant to the hospital staff."

Sara looked between Hassan and Fazil. Consultant? That

was news to her. She'd told Hassan she didn't want any payment for helping him with the clinics.

"Sara is the consultant. She's going to be helping me set up the clinics. I'm sure HR informed you of her volunteer status."

Fazil turned his gaze to her. His dark, beady eyes made her think of a river rat. "Fine. You know how I feel about adding to the hospital's budget."

"An old argument." Hassan sighed. Sara felt for him. It was difficult to get the money people to understand what was needed. "Right now, I want to get to the bottom of why Rahma is being rude to Izza."

"I told you, Dr. Hassan. Izza is lazy. She must be directed to do everything. If I don't keep on top of her, then nothing gets done."

Rahma's whiney voice grated on Sara's nerves. She lifted her head and glanced around the floor. At the nurses' station were two nurses not doing anything but talking. Sara wrinkled her nose. She nudged Hassan and tilted her head that direction.

"I see two of the floor nurses at their station doing nothing. Why are you not talking to them?"

Sara hid a grin as Rahma's mouth opened and then closed.

"It doesn't matter," Fazil said. "Rahma is in charge of the nurses."

The hair on the back of Sara's neck bristled. Something

was out of place here. Hassan's arm tightened around her waist.

"She is, but being rude to them isn't going to help us keep good staff." He glared at the pair. "Izza will be temporarily assigned to Sara starting this afternoon. That is all." He guided Sara away from the pair and to the elevator.

Sara didn't say a word until they were enclosed alone in the elevator. "Well, that wasn't pleasant."

"I'm sorry." He drew his free hand through his hair. "Rahma and Fazil can be a bit much."

"It's more than that."

"Yes." The doors opened on the second floor, and he escorted her out. "Let's go into the cafeteria and talk."

"All right." Sara was curious. It was apparent Fazil didn't like Hassan's actions, but there was something deeper. Something she couldn't quite put her finger on.

Hassan led Sara over to the coffee urns and poured them each a cup. "Do you want something to eat?"

"This is fine." She took the mug from his fingers and added cream to it.

He stared at the amount of cream she added. When she looked up and saw him looking at her, she grinned. "I always have a little coffee with my cream."

A chuckle left his lips, and he led her over to a table in

the corner where they could have some privacy. "Fazil is a pain," he commented, waiting for her to sit before taking his own seat.

Sara took a sip of her coffee before setting the cup on the table. "I gathered that." She toyed with the handle. "But there's something more."

"Yes." He let out a sigh. His gut tightened. Warm fingers caressed the back of his hand, and he turned his hand over until her fingers rested against his palms, her touch helping him stay grounded. "He's also the secondary minister of health."

"Secondary minister of health?"

"Yes, we have various ministers to help the royal family." He ran his fingers over hers. "I'm the primary minister of health, but Fazil has a say."

"Wasn't Omar, the guy that tried to hurt Catherine, a minister?"

"He was." Hassan paused. "Fazil can be a good man, but he's older. He wants to continue the old ways, which are not working. So we clash."

"He's protective." She'd seen this before, older workers fearing the younger generation.

"Old ideals, not protectiveness. Tell me, what did you smell when Fazil approached us?"

"Wildflowers. I thought it unusual, but maybe he was wearing cologne."

Hassan shook his head. "We have an opium problem in Bashir."

"Opium? Or opiates?" She sat back but kept her hand in contact with his.

"I'm sure you're aware that opiates are made from opium."

"Of course. I'm trying to understand."

"The older generation sees no problem in smoking opium. While we haven't made it illegal as of yet, Fazil is one of them who smokes it."

"But smoking it is as addictive as taking the pills."

"It is. That's the reason for the drug rehabilitation clinic, but also why I need more outreach clinics in the villages."

"That makes sense."

"Fazil is totally against them." Hassan took a drink of his coffee. "With my being busy here at the hospital with my patients, our father's heart attack, Malik and Catherine's romance, and then Omar trying to scare Catherine away, I'm normally more vigilant than this." He rubbed his chin. "I should confront him on the issue."

"Not today." Her eyes held understanding and compassion. "You've been busy. I have a question."

Hassan nodded. He'd have a million, but Sara grasped things pretty quickly. "How many doctors and nurses do you have?"

"I don't feel there are enough. We have the adult wing, the children's wing, an entire surgical floor, ICU, the new drug addiction wing, and two walk-in clinics. HR is on the first floor, along with offices on the upper floors for the doctors, changing rooms and showers if needed on the upper floors." He closed his eyes. "I believe we have ten doctors, two surgeons, and twenty nurses."

"That's not nearly enough."

He curled his fingers around Sara's. "What are you thinking?"

"Can I look at the staffing records?"

"You have access from your office computer."

"There was no computer in the office I was given. In fact, there wasn't anything but a desk, a chair, and an empty file cabinet."

"Damn it," he swore softly. "I told them to give you a fully furnished office."

"It's not your fault."

"I'll get you a computer and have it hooked up right away." What the heck was going on? It was like Fazil wanted him to fail. Fazil didn't have to like what he was doing, but it was for the good of the people.

"That's fine. In the meantime, are there files I can go through without causing a ruckus?"

"Yes, but it will be slow."

"With Izza's help, I should be able to make some progress. Let me go through them and see what I find."

"I'm not happy about this."

"Hassan, this isn't your fault. You're a doctor, your

patients come first."

"I'm part of the royal family."

Sara nodded. "And you're also looking out for the people of Bashir. Do you have a plan for opening the outreach clinics and the rehab unit?"

"Yes. I'll make sure you have a copy of that as well." He liked how her mind worked. She was bright and caught onto things quickly.

"Good." She disentangled her fingers from his and picked up her coffee. "Let's finish up our coffee and get to work. I have a feeling there's a lot to be done."

Hassan's mood lightened. Sara was good for him and good to help him with the clinics.

Sara stared at the mess of the file room. "I'm hoping most of this stuff is in the computer."

Izza grimaced. "I'm afraid not. The hospital only got the computers a year ago, and the staff isn't good at using them."

Sara sighed. This was not good. "Okay, let's start sorting these files out and see what we have."

For the rest of the afternoon, Sara and Izza sorted files. There were patient files mixed in with administration orders, staffing orders, and medication orders, and all of it should have been computerized or at least scanned.

This was so not good. Sara didn't want to add to Hassan's

burdens, but there was going to be some office help and computers needed to get all this done. Plus she wanted to figure out why the staff wasn't using the computers.

She'd talked with Izza, who was comfortable using the computer and did, but then Izza said she also had to make handwritten notes on paper. She explained a lot of the nurses hated doing both, so they only did the one they were told to do—the handwritten notes.

Sara stretched out the kinks in her back and glanced at her watch. "Oh, my goodness, it's after six. Izza, why didn't you say something? Shouldn't you be off shift by now?" She was dismayed she'd kept Izza so late.

"It's okay. I like helping you and I didn't mind."

"We still need to call it a day." Izza had been a great help today; she had a quick mind and a knack for this type of work. And the laziness Rahma had commented on was nonexistent.

Sara gathered up her notes and several files. She wanted to read up on Rahma and some of the hospital staff. Maybe she could figure out what was going on. Together, she and Izza left the room.

She made sure the door was locked behind them. This was another thing she needed to discuss with Hassan. The door had been unlocked and the keys left inside the room. Anyone could have walked into the file room and taken what they wanted, including confidential files. Sara dropped the keys into her pocket for safekeeping.

"Let's meet here tomorrow at nine if that works for you?" she said to Izza.

"That's fine. I usually work eight to five. I can come in at eight and do some work before you arrive."

Sara frowned. "Izza, I don't want you to get overworked. You will tell me if this is too much."

Izza grinned. "I'm fine, Lady Sara. I enjoy nursing, but helping you is fun too. I'm learning a lot." Izza waved before she walked away.

Sara shook her head, then went to the main desk. The older woman there was able to tell her where Hassan was. Sara made her way to the adult floor and stood outside a hospital room.

Hassan spoke to a man lying in the bed. His wife sat in a chair next to the bed, and they were holding hands. The woman looked up and saw Sara. Hassan turned around.

"I'm sorry," Sara said. "I didn't mean to disturb you. I'm getting ready to leave."

"Are you Dr. Hassan's girlfriend?" the older woman asked.

"Now, Amirah," Hassan said, "you need to concentrate on your husband, not my love life."

The woman laughed as Hassan moved to the doorway where Sara stood. "What love life? You need a woman, like King Malik found. A good woman."

Hassan shook his head. "Can you give me five minutes and then we can go home together?" he asked Sara.

"You don't have to leave. I'll be fine on my own."

Hassan ran a finger down her cheek, and Sara shivered from his touch. "You will wait for me," he said in a low tone. Her blood heated in her veins.

She nodded and backed away from his touch. She made her way to the nurses' station. It was empty. That didn't surprise her. She needed to talk with Hassan and Malik about staffing. She wanted to discuss a strategy on how to staff the hospital better.

Sara walked around the desk and began looking at the equipment. Computers were there but not turned on. Files were lined up in neat little stands, so that was a plus. At least the station was neat and clean. She heard footsteps and glanced up.

"Sorry you had to wait."

"No worries." She slipped out from behind the desk.

Hassan slipped his arm around her waist and guided her to the elevator. His touch made her skin sing. She really did enjoy his little touches. Within a few minutes they were outside and the car was waiting from them. "How is it that the car is waiting for us?"

"I called Najah and let him know we were ready to go home." Hassan opened the door for her to climb in.

"Sneaky," she said, sliding into the vehicle. She sat the files and her pad on the seat between them.

"Some light reading tonight?" He shut the car door and put his hand on the files.

"A bit." She swallowed. "I would like to talk with you and Malik, since he's now the king."

"About?" He kept his tone light, but there was a question in his eyes.

"The hospital." She ran her fingers over his arm before retreating. "I hate to burden you with this."

"What did you find today?" He rubbed his forehead, and Sara saw the lines of worry there. She reached up and captured his hand with hers.

"I don't want you to worry. You can't do everything." And he couldn't. Maybe she could get him to realize that. Just because he was the minister of health and a doctor didn't mean he could do it all.

"I'm aware of that."

"Good, because I don't want you going off half-cocked." She threw him a grin.

"I can't promise that, but I will try."

"Okay." She nodded. "The file room was unlocked. I found a set of keys in the room. It is locked now and I have the key. Is there more than one key? If not, we need to return to the hospital."

"Fazil should have one and so should HR." His fingers rubbed her knuckles. "It should not have been unlocked."

"The file room is in total disarray."

"How can that be?" His lips turned down. "Six months ago people were hired to get it cleaned up."

"I'm not sure, but it's been longer than six months since

anyone touched anything. Hassan, do you use computers to log in your patient information?"

"Yes, of course. Two years ago we modernized to the computers. I know some of the staff are not comfortable with them. We've done classes to help them." The lines on his forehead increased.

Sara reached up and smoothed those lines with her fingers. "I talked with Izza today, and she said most of the staff don't use the computers. There might be some, but I'm not sure how things are working out. When you came out from visiting the couple, I was behind the nurse's station."

"I noticed. As for the computers." He rubbed the back of his neck. "All my notes and the notes from the nurses I've worked with are in there."

"There was no one at the nurses station. The computers were off, and there were files neatly stacked with patients' names on them." She paused. She hated adding to his burdens. "Anyone could have walked up to the desk and accessed patient information."

Hassan swore. "This is unacceptable. Everyone should be using the computers."

"Hassan." She squeezed his hand. "People don't change overnight, but I think more training might be in order."

"But there's more." He sighed, frustration written all over his face.

"Yes." The car pulled up to the palace. "After dinner we can discuss this with Malik?"

"Of course. That is a good idea." Hassan opened the door, and they climbed out. When they walked in the front door, Anna was waiting for them, her hands on her hips.

"It's about time. Didn't I tell you dinner was at seven?" Anna said.

Hassan ducked his head, and Sara had to fight a grin. "I'm sorry, Anna. It's my fault, I was busy and lost track of time." It wasn't a lie.

"More likely my son was caught up with a patient, and that is not a bad thing. But he works too hard and too much." Her gaze bounced between the two of them. "Now go get cleaned up and meet us in the dining room. Both of you." Anna marched off.

"We'd better be quick. I don't want to upset mama bear," Sara said.

Hassan laughed. He took the files from her and set them on a side table. "For after dinner. Now let's go." He took her by the hand and led her up the stairs.

After dinner, Sara squirmed against the leather chair in Malik's office. She was the one who had asked for the meeting, and there was nothing to be nervous about.

"Hassan said you wanted to talk about the hospital and clinics."

"Yes." She swallowed. "I wanted to ask about bringing in

a few people to teach the nursing staff how to use the computers. I'm pretty sure most of the doctors are okay with them, but if not, them too." Her words came out in a rush.

"I thought everyone was trained?" Malik frowned.

"Me too," Hassan said. "But as Sara found out today, some of the nurses aren't using them. They're using the old paper files."

"And that's another point. The old paper files need to be digitized."

"Fazil doesn't seem to be doing his job," Malik commented.

"I don't want to get anyone into trouble or step on any toes," Sara said. "There just seems to be no oversight, and that's no one's fault."

"It's Fazil's," Malik said. "We trust him to run the hospital properly and see to it things are done. That's his job."

"Fazil is smoking opium again," Hassan commented.

"That is unacceptable. How could you tell?" Malik asked.

"He reeked of it." Hassan ran a hand through his hair.

"I noticed the smell of wildflowers. I thought it was odd until Hassan told me." Sara sat back in her chair. So far things were going smoothly.

"I'll visit Fazil tomorrow. He's been warned." Malik reached for his phone. "Is ten in the morning okay with you, Hassan?"

"Yes. What are you planning, Malik?" Hassan leaned forward.

"He'll get one more warning, directly from me. I will make it clear that this is his last warning."

"You know he'll deny it," Hassan said as his fingers tapped on the arm of the chair.

"Yes, but that doesn't mean I don't have my ways." Malik typed into his phone. "Is there more?"

Sara looked at Hassan, who nodded. They'd talked briefly before the meeting, but she wasn't sure about approaching Malik about what she'd seen.

"Please, Sara, tell me your concerns," Malik encouraged.

"Okay, this was just what I observed today. The lead nurse, Rahma, doesn't understand the concept of staffing or what needs to be accomplished. She's rude to the younger nurses while allowing the older nurses to do anything they want."

Malik leaned forward, laying his arms on his desk. "Tell me more."

"The children's floor had two nurses at the station doing nothing but talking, but Rahma verbally admonished the nurse, Izza, who Hassan sent to help me. And then when I went to the adult floor, there were no nurses at the station at all."

Hassan shifted in his chair, and Sara peeked at him from the corner of her eye. He didn't look happy, and she couldn't blame him.

"That is not good," Malik said, then again picked up his pen and began writing.

"No, and I wasn't aware of it," Hassan mentioned.

"And why should you be?" Sara touched the back of Hassan's hand where it rested on the chair. "You're a doctor." She looked at Malik. "If you want to get clinics up and running, the hospital needs to be at top speed. Most of the clinics are not set up to take care of major problems and they would be sent to the hospital, but if the hospital staff isn't up to the job, errors and deaths can occur."

"Hassan, opinion?" Malik asked.

"Sara is right. We have enough trouble with the older population understanding preventive care is important."

"And the opium problems are not helping." Malik sat back and rubbed his chin.

"Opium issues? Does that mean Fazil isn't the only one with the addiction at the hospital?" Sara's stomach clenched. She, of all people, understood how addicting opiates were, since she had once been addicted herself.

"At the hospital, he's probably the only one," Malik said. "Bashir City is a large and bustling metropolis, but most of our older people live on the edge of the city limits or in the villages. We have other minor cities, and we've been working at getting people involved. But the poppy growers have taken over the northeast section of the country."

"How did this happen?" She wondered how the poppy growers had been allowed to flourish.

"Short version is our grandfather let them," Malik said.

"We've confined them to the northeast as we've grown as a country, but it's still a concern."

"I'm not blaming anyone."

Hassan curled his fingers around hers. "We know. We blame ourselves, we haven't been able to move fast enough in eradicating them."

"As fast as we work to grow our economy and build relationships, the opium trade keeps going," Malik said.

"I get it. So the clinics, where do you have them now?"

"One on the outskirts of Bashir City, which is staffed, and one in a village to the northeast, where a doctor and nurse go out every couple of months," Hassan said.

Sara frowned. "Two for a population as large as Bashir's ... Okay, I can see there's lots of work to be done."

"Yes. We want at least one clinic in each region, if not more, plus more than just a small walk-in clinic at the hospital," Hassan said, giving her hand a squeeze.

Sara exhaled. "I have my work cut out for me. I'll start working out some business plans for not only training current staff, but new staff, and lists of what will be needed at the clinics—not only equipment but personnel. Let's just say everything."

"That's a lot for one person to take on," Malik said.

Sara grinned. "I can handle it."

Hassan smiled and shook hands with the dignitaries attending the official engagement party for Malik and Catherine Saturday night. He kept one eye on the doorway. Where was Sara? Catherine assured him she'd arrive in due time.

The last person in line walked away and Hassan turned ... he froze. Sara stood in the doorway. Her blonde hair was piled on top of her head in an elaborate style, but what caught his attention was her beautiful skin.

The emerald green dress was held up by two tiny straps over her shoulders, exposing lots of creamy skin. A small gold necklace with a pendant at the end encased her neck, making it look longer. His gaze continued down. The fabric hugged her generous breasts, then at her waist flared out a bit before flowing down to the floor.

"If you don't rush to her side now, you'll lose her to one of those other guys," Rafi said, nudging him in the back.

Hassan didn't spare his brother a glance. He crossed the room to Sara. Her eyes widened when he stopped in front of her. "Lady Sara." He took her hand in his, raising it to his lips and kissing the back of it.

"Prince Hassan." Her voice was soft and hesitant.

He fought against grinning. "So formal," he said in a quiet tone. He drew her arm through his and led her into the ballroom.

"Catherine said in public like this I should use it." Her fingers tightened on his arm. "I really shouldn't be here."

"You are Catherine's maid of honor at the wedding. So, yes, you should be here. Catherine expects you to be here. Relax and enjoy."

"Easy for you to say, I feel on display."

His gaze took in the room. Yes, the men were looking at her like she was a delicious treat, and the women were staring at him. Well, he was used to that. "The men can't believe your beauty."

A giggle left her lips, and her hold on him relaxed. "Are you flirting with me?"

"More than that." He drew her to the side. "Would it bother you if I wanted more than just some fun flirting?"

Sara looked around the room, then her gaze came back to his. "Hassan, is this the right place?"

"You can't run away or hide here." He kept his stance relaxed but made sure no one was close to them.

"I was working," she said, her voice soft.

"Too much." He raised his hand and his fingers touched her creamy cheek. "You were at the hospital at seven in the morning until almost eight at night for the last two days. I call that hiding."

She ducked her head. "I wanted to have a business plan on the clinics ready."

"Was that all?"

"Yes, you said professional on the job, that's what I was doing."

Hassan silently cursed himself. Yes, he did tell her they

would be professional at the hospital, but he didn't mean they couldn't spend time together. "I did. But tonight we're just Hassan and Sara."

"A little hard since you're here in your official capacity as a prince."

"All eyes will be on Malik and Catherine." He nodded to where the pair stood across the room, surrounded by not only dignitaries but the press as well.

"I guess you are right. What did you have in mind?" Her green eyes flashed with desire.

The music started, and a few couples took the dance floor. His arm slipped around her waist. "Dance with me." He swept her out onto the dance floor.

Sara's heart pounded as Hassan pulled her into his arms. What was it about him? She'd met handsome men, even rich ones, but Hassan ... there was something about him that melted her bones and her mind and called to her submissive side.

Hassan was a superb dancer; he guided her around the floor with ease. Tonight, she'd let her fears around having a relationship with Hassan float away. She wanted to be with him, even if it was for a short time.

"I want to kiss you so much," he said in a husky voice on their fourth dance.

A thrill of excitement shot through her veins. She wanted his lips on hers, to taste him, to know his kisses.

"What's stopping you?" Holy crap, where did those words

come from? She usually wasn't that bold, especially with a dominant.

His chuckle reached her ears. "If we weren't in the middle of a dance floor, with not only my family but paparazzi and dignitaries all over the place, I'd strip you bare and kiss you all over."

Her knees grew weak. "So, if we were alone, you wouldn't hesitate."

His arms tightened around her waist. He danced them over to the open patio doors. Once they were outside, he stopped dancing and guided her across the patio and down the stairs.

She didn't say a word as he led her away from the lights and music into the depths of the garden until they came to a gazebo. The moon was bright, illuminating the gazebo as Hassan tugged her up the three stairs and inside the structure.

He pulled her to a stop, and she raised her gaze to his. His dark blue eyes were filled with passion. Sara opened her mouth. He pulled her close, and he lowered his head until his lips were on hers.

Desire flared deep in her belly, and she leaned into the kiss. His lips were firm against hers as his tongue swept into her mouth. How long had it been since she'd kissed someone? Well, they had kissed earlier this week, but nothing like this.

Her body was coming alive under his kiss as if it were

awakening from a long sleep. It probably was. After Peter's betrayal, she'd barely dated, but now she was ready to jump in head first.

Hassan's hands rested in the small of her back, and she wound her arms around his neck, toying with his silky hair. One of his hands slid up her back to her neck when he broke the kiss.

He rested his forehead against hers as his fingers trailed over her bare shoulder, past the hollow of her throat to the top of her dress just above her breasts. A path of fire followed his touch. She wanted more, so much more.

"Please," she whispered.

"I so want to please you." His tone was soft and deep, sending shivers of awareness over her skin. His palm covered her breast over the fabric.

Sara let out a moan. His caress was tender and exciting.

"You like that?"

"Yes." Her breath puffed out in rapid pulses.

"And this?" He pinched her nipple.

Sara gasped and pushed closer to him. Heat and a zing of lust swept from her nipple straight to her core. Muscles contracted with pure pleasure.

"I think you did." His free hand cupped the nape of her neck, holding her firm. "Do you like to play in the bedroom, my Sara?"

His question sent a fission of discovery into her brain. Her submissive side was reacting to his words, his tone, his voice. It had been a long time since she'd felt this way. "I do." The words came out hesitantly. She was laying herself open to him.

"I do too." His breath was hot against the skin of her face. "I'm a dominant in the bedroom. Do you know what that means?"

Her knees grew weak at his question. "Yes."

"Such a wonderful gift you give me." His hand slid from her breast to her waist. He stared into her eyes, and she met his gaze. "Right now isn't the time or place to discuss this, but I want to explore this attraction with you."

A tremor swept through her body. "And I want to explore with you." She wasn't going to deny her needs anymore. They could be professional on the job.

Hassan groaned and closed his eyes, and then reopened them. Flames of passion flared in his gaze. "Tonight, after we're done with this party, leave your balcony door unlocked, and I'll come to you."

Sara swallowed. It was hard for her to leave any door unlocked. "I'll do my best." That's all she could promise.

His lips captured hers once again, and when they broke apart their harsh breathing filled the air.

"We'd better get back before we're missed," he said.

She nodded. She'd rather stay in the gazebo with him, but if they stayed, eventually someone would come looking for them. Probably Catherine.

"Later we'll continue this." He turned, and keeping his

arm around her waist, he guided her from the gazebo and up the path. He paused before leading her through the double doors leading to the ballroom. "When we walk back in, keep your head up and smile. Don't worry that people might be staring at us."

"What?" The sensual haze cleared her brain.

"Don't get flustered." His hands framed her face. "As far as anyone is concerned, we just took a walk in the garden to cool off after dancing."

"I can handle that." She'd never thought about people thinking she and Hassan had escaped for a romantic tryst.

"I know you can." He dropped a kiss on her nose, then took her hand, and they walked back inside.

"You and Hassan were gone for a while," Catherine said, smiling at Sara five minutes later.

"It wasn't all that long."

"The press is buzzing already, so you better get prepared."

"What?" Sara glanced around. She didn't see anyone lurking nearby. "Any advice?"

"I ignore them as much as possible when they start asking personal questions. You do have one advantage I don't."

"What's that?"

"Hassan is the third son. I had to pick the king."

"This from the woman who told me not to get involved with a royal."

Catherine laughed. "It was a friendly warning, but I knew that wasn't going to work. You and Hassan could light up a whole country together from the sparks you throw off each other."

Sara ducked her head. She couldn't dispute Catherine's words. Sara's gaze collided with Hassan's, and he winked at her. "So what do you suggest?" She could use some advice.

"Enjoy yourself," Catherine said in a quiet voice. "Don't let the press worry you. Have fun and let the relationship take you wherever it does. You deserve to be happy."

Sara smiled. "I'll do my best."

"You'd better." Catherine swatted at Sara's arm. "I'd love to have my best friend become a part of my new family."

"We've always been family." Sara's stomach clenched. Could she be part of this royal family? It was too early to tell. She wanted to explore her attraction to Hassan and see where it led.

Several hours later, Sara paced around her spacious sitting room, unable to settle down. As Hassan had requested, she'd unlocked the balcony doors fifteen minutes ago. Her nerves were dancing an Irish jig along her skin.

It had been a long time since she'd been this nervous and even longer since she'd had someone to play with. While she wasn't sure how kinky he was, she'd find out tonight. Talking was the first step.

A knock on the window made her spin around as the balcony handle turned. Hassan slipped through the opening, closed the door, and locked it. Gone was the formal suit; now he was dressed in a pair of black jeans and a white shirt. His feet were bare. When her gaze lifted to his face, he was smiling.

"Why don't we get comfortable to talk?" He gestured to the small sofa.

Sara nodded and her throat grew dry. She hadn't been this nervous around him before, so she tried to figure out why she was now. Maybe because they were about to talk about a relationship. Possibly a kinky relationship.

She sat down and waited until Hassan took a seat next to her before turning to face him.

"You look nervous," he said as his fingers pushed back a lock of her hair.

She turned her face into his touch. "I am."

"Tonight we are just going to talk or negotiate, does that help?"

The word negotiate sent flitters through her stomach.

"To start with what I said in the gazebo. I'm a bedroom Dom. In the bedroom I expect your submission, your obedience. Outside the bedroom, I may say things that rub you the wrong way because I'm protective and want to make sure you are safe and taken care of." His fingers slid from her cheek to trail down her throat.

"I can do that." Sara swallowed. His touch was distracting and yet comforting.

"How much experience with kink do you have?"

"A bit." She bit the inside of her cheek. Honesty and consent in all things kink, she reminded herself. "I started playing when I was twenty-three. I went to a club and found a Dom who was willing to mentor me."

"Why a club?"

"Because, for me, it wasn't about sex." Her gaze slid away from his face. Why was this so hard for her? Maybe because she wanted Hassan in a way she hadn't wanted any other man, and it scared her.

"Sara." He cupped her chin, his palm warm against her skin. He lifted her face and waited until her gaze met his. "No judgment from me."

"I'm a nurse, and as you probably know, the pressure and emotional toll were atrocious." Hassan nodded, but questions filled his gaze. "Doctors have it worse. I needed someplace I could let go of everything. I could cry, scream, and yell, and no one would think anything of it unless I said my safe word."

He nodded. "Control does that for me. It allows me to channel my emotions into pleasure for my partner."

"Good point. So I played for two years; it helped me rid

myself of the toxins from the job." And from old fears, but that could come later.

"When did you stop going to the club?"

"Three years ago." Her stomach clenched. If it hadn't been for Catherine ... no, she wasn't going back to that dark place.

"What made you stop?"

"An ex-boyfriend." She'd been so stupid to trust Peter. She saw it now, all his little manipulations, his put-downs, his trying to isolate her. "Catherine and I were flatmates when I met Peter. While I never moved in with him, we were practically living together toward the end of our relationship."

"So you had sex with Peter, but went to the club to let go of your control."

She nodded. There was another reason, but she didn't want to reveal it right now. "Peter found out about the club and insisted on going with me one night. Taking him was a mistake."

"He didn't understand."

"I wish it had been only that. Unknown to me, Peter was doing drugs. He was a doctor, and I understood the pressure, but drugs are not the answer. That night we went to the club, he'd taken several different ones. He was higher than a kite, but I didn't notice. So when my Dom went to help me release my tension, Peter went crazy."

A shiver swept up her spine, remembering that night.

How Peter ran to her, his fingers clawing at the restraints as the club monitors tried to pull him off. The way her Dom stared at her with disappointment in his eyes while he undid the restraints. Then the owner of the club having to come out and help. One hell of a mess.

"How did your Dom help you release that upset Peter so much?"

"Flogging."

Hassan nodded, his gaze holding hers. "This Peter was told of the rules of the club and not to interrupt." He released her chin.

"Yes." Sara sat back and ran her hands over her cold arms. "Since I was a member he was my responsibility. I pulled on my street clothes, and with the help of the monitors, got Peter out the door and into a cab. The entire way to his flat he ranted and raved. I ignored him. But once we got inside his place ... " An icy shiver danced over her spine, and she hunched her shoulders as it made its way up her neck.

"Did he physically hurt you?" Hassan's voice was tight and low.

She shook her head. "Not really. He did slap me, but I slapped him right back."

"Good girl." There was a smile in his voice.

Sara lifted her head. "Peter didn't take it so well. He accused me of all sorts of things, threatened to out me and the club."

Shock flashed across Hassan's face. "Did he?"

"No. Mainly because I threatened to out his drug habit or, should I say, addiction. I hadn't seen it coming, he'd kept it hidden from me. I'd caught him when we first got together, but he swore he quit. I missed the signs."

"It happens to the best of us." Hassan rubbed her arms in a soothing motion.

"Anyway, I went back a couple of days later to the club to apologize and let them know I wouldn't be back. My Dom had already moved on, so there was no loss for him."

"But you were lost."

"A bit. I changed jobs because Peter and I worked at the same hospital." She fought to keep her tone steady. "Peter would make snide comments about my work, then tell my boss I wasn't doing my job."

Hassan's hands stilled on her arms, tension radiating from him.

"It wasn't pleasant. But he wouldn't let up. So with my boss's help, I was able to transfer to a sister hospital."

"What happened to this Peter?"

"Last I heard, he'd been caught using drugs on the job, and they fired him on the spot." A bit of satisfaction had flowed through her on hearing that news.

"Good. I hope the man rots in hell."

A grin crossed Sara's lips. "By that time I was working with Dr. Doom."

"Dr. Doom?" Laughter filled his voice as his hands relaxed.

"Nickname, but that's another story." Looking back, with some distance between her and the job, it had been the best thing to happen to her. She'd been burning out between being a nurse and working on her administrator degree.

"I will accept that. I have also been to a club, so we're on the same page. Tell me what your hard limits are?"

Sara shifted. "I'm pretty much toward the light end of the BDSM scale. I like flogging, spanking, and toys. I'm not into pain or heavy-duty stuff."

"Understood." He tilted his head, and a lock of his dark hair fell onto his forehead. "We're compatible. As you can understand, this will stay private between us. If the press were to get ahold of what we do privately, it would reflect badly on the family."

"Of course." She hadn't thought of that. "Being in the public eye must be trying at times."

A small smile tilted his lips. "Not as bad for me as it is for Malik and Catherine. I'm sure you noticed when you were out with Catherine."

"Yes. She's doing great at dealing with them and the bodyguards."

"We're not off the hook though."

"What?"

"Our foray into the garden was noticed, and the press was already buzzing about it. They're going to pick up we're an item."

"I can handle it." She'd learned how to ignore the press when they'd had critical situations at the hospital.

"I believe you can." His hands closed over her shoulders. "Our playtime will be confined to the palace."

"Are you telling me you have a playroom here?" Catherine hadn't mentioned that.

Hassan grinned. "No, but my suite is more than big enough to make sure we can play."

A shiver of anticipation slid through her veins. She couldn't wait to explore with him.

"Our first time will be soon. Not tonight."

"Why not?"

"Because it is late, and we both need rest." His eyes brightened. "What is your safe word?"

"I always used the club standards."

"I'd rather be a little more creative than that. While I know most people won't say those words during play, I prefer special words."

She tilted her head and thought for a moment. "How about 'camel' for slow down and 'fox' to stop?"

"Creative." He was silent for a moment. "Those will work. I will check in with you often to see how you're doing."

She nodded. While her Dom at the club had usually checked in on her, it was more to make sure she was still with him than anything else.

"This will be a relationship, Sara." Hassan's gaze captured her. "While we will play, sex is also on the table."

Her core clenched, and she nodded.

"Words, sweetheart."

"That is acceptable."

"So formal." He leaned down and brushed a kiss over her lips. "It is getting late." He stood and helped her to her feet. "I have to make early rounds at the hospital tomorrow, but after that I believe we have a meeting with Malik about the clinics."

"Yes." He drew her over to the balcony doors. "I have a plan all drawn up and ready to discuss," she said.

"I look forward to it." They stood facing each other.

"Why do you use the balcony doors?" she asked.

"Privacy." He slid his arms around her waist and tugged her close. "Why do you insist on having the doors locked?"

Sara shook her head. "It's just one of those things." Old fears crowded her mind.

"Very well." He brushed another soft kiss over her lips before he turned, unlocked the doors, and opened one. "Until tomorrow, sweetheart."

Hassan slipped out the door and pulled it shut behind him. Sara locked the door, then lifted her fingers to her lips. Her skin tingled from his touch. She reminded herself she and Hassan were just starting out. Yes, they were attracted to each other, but for right now, she was going see where this led and not go too deep. She couldn't wait until they could play together and see how they meshed.

4

Late Sunday morning, Sara found herself once again in Malik's office with Hassan. She'd laid out her plans for the clinics.

"That sounds reasonable and effective," Malik said.

"What about Fazil?" Hassan asked.

Sara grimaced. "He's not going to like it."

"This will come from me," Malik said. "As king, I need to see this is done for the people. If he has any objections, he can voice them to me and me only."

Hassan grinned, and Sara's breath caught in her throat. Until that moment she'd only seen Malik the man, but now he was the king.

"I would like to see the clinic in Bashir City and, with

permission, start putting out feelers for staff for the clinics," Sara said.

"Staffing will be the hardest task. Do you have ideas about that?" Malik asked.

"Yes, as I mentioned before, incentives could work. I plan to use those to help staff the clinics, but also use the resources here. I understand there is a new batch of nurses who live in Bashir arriving in the next few weeks."

"I'd forgotten." Hassan sat forward. "We usually use them at the hospital."

"That would be good training to start with, but as we open clinics, see who would like to help with the clinics. If some of the nurses are from the villages we put clinics in, that's a plus."

"You seem to have thought of everything," Malik said, leafing through her report.

"I tried."

"Good. Let me call Khalid in here. We need to talk security." Hassan let out a groan, and Malik laughed. "A necessary evil, brother. You haven't seen the morning papers, have you?"

"No." Hassan looked at Sara. Her cheeks became pink. "You have?"

"Catherine was delighted to show them to me."

Malik picked up his phone. "Khalid, my office please, and bring the morning paper for Hassan to see."

Within a few minutes, Khalid arrived and handed Hassan

the paper. At first glance, Hassan saw a picture of Malik and Catherine surrounded by the family, then he scanned further down. There was a picture of him and Sara right after they had returned from the garden.

He had been gazing down at her face and she had been looking up at him. The contented look on both their faces surprised him. He read the caption, "Has the Crown Princess's best friend captured Prince Hassan's attention? We shall see."

"Great," Hassan muttered, tossing the paper onto Malik's desk.

"Don't stress over it," Sara said. "It's no big deal."

Hassan couldn't believe how calm she was with all the attention, but in a way she was right. The press would get bored quickly.

"I'm assuming you didn't call me in here just to talk about the press?" Khalid said.

"No." Malik outlined the plan for the clinics.

"We will need more security." Khalid leaned against the wall.

"Agreed. What can I help with?" Malik asked.

"I've already put out some feelers. How do you feel about ex-military from the UK and US?"

Malik rubbed his chin. "Sounds like a good idea. They'll be good and already trained."

"Yes," Khalid said. "I'll start recruiting them."

"We have a plan then." Malik sat back in his chair.

"When can we go to the Bashir City clinic?" Sara asked.

"Tomorrow." Hassan took her hand in his and squeezed it.

Hassan glanced up as Sara walked into the foyer Monday morning. They hadn't had much time alone on Sunday, but then he hadn't expected them to. After their talk with Malik, Sara had gone to find Catherine, while he'd stayed and talked security details.

Today, they'd go to the Bashir City clinic after a stop at the hospital. But Khalid had already warned him about the press.

"Good morning," Sara said.

"Morning." Hassan leaned down and brushed a kiss over her lips. He wanted to do more, but now was not the time or place.

He slipped his arm around her waist and guided her to the car. Once they were on their way, he turned to her. "I have to warn you."

"About what?"

Her blonde hair framed her face, making her green eyes appear bright, almost like shining emeralds. Hassan pushed back his desire to ravish her in the back seat. Later, he told himself.

"We made the morning papers again." It had been a grainy shot, one taken at a great distance.

"Oh?" She looked surprised.

"It was a shot someone got of us walking around yesterday afternoon with Catherine."

"Are you upset?"

"No. Why would you think that?" He wasn't, but his need to protect her pushed at him.

"Because you seem a tad off this morning, as if you're angry."

"No, I ... " He broke off as the car turned to the entrance of the hospital. It was crowded with people.

"What's going on?" Sara asked, staring out the window.

"Damn," he muttered. "I was hoping it wouldn't have started yet."

"What?" Sara's eyes grew wide as people pushed against the vehicle.

"This is a result of the photos in the press. They jump to speculation."

"And this is the result?" She waved her hand at the sea of people.

"Yes."

"And you didn't think to warn me before now?" She shook her head. "You let me wear jeans."

Hassan laughed and took her hand in his. "You look beautiful and perfect. There is no reason to worry." The door opened next to Hassan. He released her hand and climbed out of the vehicle, then he turned and held a hand out to her.

He was proud of her when she slipped her hand into his and allowed him to help her from the car. Flashes from the cameras went off, and she leaned back. Hassan slipped his arm around her waist to guide her as Najah and two other bodyguards cleared the way.

"So, who is the lady in your life, Prince Hassan?" a reporter yelled.

"Are you two an item?" another yelled.

"Does this mean there's going to be a double royal wedding?" yet another yelled.

Sara's head swiveled to the reporter after the last question. "No comment," Hassan said. He kept moving forward until they were in the elevator with Najah.

"What the heck was that about a double royal wedding?"

He shook his head. "They're just speculating."

"About us? I've only been here a week."

"Sara." Hassan turned to her and cupped her face. "I told you about the speculation."

"You did, but this?" Her hand shook when she raised it to place over his. "I didn't expect people to flock around us. It's crazy."

"Welcome to the world of the royal family."

Najah laughed. Sara glared at him. "I'm sorry, my lady, but Prince Hassan is right. The moment they saw the two of you together on the dance floor Saturday night they started putting two and two together."

"And came up with five." Sara let out a laugh.

"Of course." Hassan leaned down. "Time for the professional face," he said, stepping back from her as the elevator doors opened. "One hour and then we'll leave for the clinic."

Sara nodded. "Let's just hope they've given up by then."

Two hours later, they drove into Bashir City. While Hassan wanted to drive all the way to the clinic, Sara insisted they walk part of the way. She wanted to absorb the atmosphere of the area and take the temperature of the people. Luckily, they'd lost most of the press while they were at the hospital.

They walked in silence, and she enjoyed how the people of Bashir interacted with Hassan. Now she understood what Catherine meant about the family being different. This wasn't an official function. Actually, it was as far from official as one could get, but Hassan stopped and talked, shook hands, and smiled with each person he could.

Najah stayed close to her side, while the other two bodyguards stayed close to Hassan. It was clear to Sara the people of Bashir loved the royal family. They'd stopped while Hassan talked to some of the men.

Sara was surprised when an older woman walked up to her. She smiled and said, "Hello."

"You are the friend to our crown princess," the woman said in broken English.

"Yes," Sara said in Arabic. "Crown Princess Catherine and I are friends."

The woman beamed at her. "You know our language."

"A bit." Sara had taken lessons with Catherine. Much to Catherine's dismay, Sara had picked up the language much faster.

"Good. You are a good match for Prince Hassan. He needs a good strong woman."

Sara's cheeks heated. "Thank you. Are you okay?" She gestured to the cane the woman was leaning on. She guessed the woman wasn't more than about sixty, but telling someone's age wasn't always easy.

"Just a little accident."

"Have you seen a doctor about it?" The woman shook her head, and Sara frowned. Hassan had told her they had issues with the older generation going to see the doctor. "Please come sit with me." Sara gestured to the bench set up against the building.

"That is very kind of you." The woman shuffled over and sat down, but the pain on her face was evident.

"Did you have a fall?" Sara asked, smiling at Najah as he stood several feet away.

"Yes."

"When did you fall? And what did you fall on?" Her nursing instincts kicked in.

"A few days ago. I stumbled in the marketplace and bruised my hip."

Sara thought for a moment. "How big of a bruise?"

The woman shrugged her shoulders, and Sara held up her hands. "Like this." She made a small circle with her fingers.

"No." The woman raised her hands and showed a large circle with them.

Sara frowned. The bruise was the size of a dinner plate. "Would you come to the clinic with me so I can see?"

The woman's eyes widened. "I'm an old woman, there is no need."

"There is every need. Do you have children?" She decided to take another tact.

"Oh, yes, and grandchildren too."

"That's wonderful. Do they live here in Bashir City?"

"My daughter does. My son, he works out in the fields."

"So he's away a lot."

The woman nodded. "He works the poppy field. I don't like it, bad things happen, but the money is good. Keeps us from losing our home, and we have food on the table. I take care of his children along with the help of his wife."

Alarm twinged Sara's senses. Hassan had told her about the opium problem. She needed to learn more. "I'm sorry, I didn't properly introduce myself. I'm Sara."

"Herma."

"Nice to meet you, Herma." A shadow fell over them, and

she looked up to see Najah standing there. "Oh, good. Najah, Herma has injured her hip and is in pain, would you please carry her to the clinic for me?"

"There is no need," Herma said.

"If my Lady Sara says there is a need, then there is, dear Herma," Najah said with respect. He reached down and lifted Herma into his arms. Another grimace of pain crossed Herma's features.

Sara looked over at Hassan. He was busy talking with several men, and she didn't want to disturb him. "Let's go to the clinic, Najah."

They walked down the street and turned the corner. The clinic building was white, and Sara frowned when she saw the open front door. When they walked in, she let out a gasp.

The waiting room was full. This didn't make sense, Hassan had told her the clinic was open six days a week with at least one doctor and one nurse on duty. Sara strode over to the makeshift reception desk, where a young girl sat playing on her phone. The girl looked up. "Have a seat, the doctor will call you when he's ready," she said before going back to her game.

"How does he know in what order to take patients?"

"I don't know. I'm only doing what I'm told."

"Told by whom?" This wasn't the way to run a clinic.

"The doctor who hired me."

Sara didn't have any authority here, but this was more

than concerning. It could be criminal. "Najah, if you'd stay here with Herma, I'll be right back."

"Lady Sara, you shouldn't be running around on your own." Najah looked around.

"There are no empty chairs. Please, Najah, I'm just going to go get Hassan, I'll be careful." Without waiting for an answer, she spun on her heel and left. She found Hassan right where she'd left him. This time she didn't hesitate to approach.

Hassan turned his head when she stopped next to him. "What is wrong?" The men around him grinned, then backed away with goodbyes. "And where is Najah?"

Sara was grateful for the privacy. "I need you at the clinic."

"That doesn't sound good." He cupped her elbow. "Is Najah at the clinic?" He nodded to the men before he guided her away, the bodyguards following.

"Yes, he's not hurt," she assured him. "Hassan, you're not going to like what you see." She'd seen Hassan at the hospital, how he was with patients. He wasn't going to be happy.

When they entered the interior of the clinic, Hassan stiffened beside her. Najah was still holding Herma in his arms. Hassan dropped his hold on Sara and marched over to the desk where the young woman sat. "Where is Dr. Saas?"

A shiver went up Sara's spine. While Hassan's voice was deep and husky, there was anger there as well.

The young woman didn't even look up from her phone.

"He's in back with a patient. You'll just have to wait your turn."

"My turn is now." He looked back at Sara. "Sara."

"Wait," the girl yelled. Hassan was walking down the hall with Sara following. "You can't go back there."

"Watch me." The bodyguards followed them down the small hallway past several open exam room doors. All empty. The last door was closed. Hassan rapped his knuckles against the door, then pushed the door open.

"What the ... "

Sara's eyes widened when Hassan moved to the side. The man who spoke was bare assed, and the woman on the exam table was nude.

Hassan turned to her. His face was closed down in anger. "Sara, would you please go out and check in with each person why they're here and how long they'd been waiting?" His voice was low.

She didn't blame him for his anger. "Of course." She spun on her heel, maneuvered around the bodyguards, and made her way back to the waiting room. The slamming of the door made her jump.

Sara stopped at the desk where the confused young lady sat. "Do you have a pad of paper and a pen?" The girl pulled open several drawers before finding them. She handed them to Sara. "Thank you," Sara said.

Hassan clenched his hands at his sides, fury vibrating through his body. "How dare you?" His voice was low and tight.

"Hassan, if you'd give me a minute—"

"You both have thirty seconds to get dressed." Hassan turned his back to allow the woman some privacy. The rustle of clothing and quiet voices of the two floated around the room.

He turned around after counting to a hundred and glared at the pair. He didn't recognize the woman, and even though she was wearing a nurse's outfit, he certainly hadn't authorized hiring her. "Where is the nurse I hired?"

"She was incompetent. I hire my own staff."

"Yes, I can see how that worked out." Hassan fought to rein in his temper. "Dr. Saas, you are now on unpaid leave, and so is the nurse. You are both to leave here now."

"Hassan, really," Dr. Saas started. "There is no reason for this."

"No reason?" Hassan clenched his teeth, willing himself not to punch this guy in the face. "There is a room full of patients, a receptionist that has no idea of what to do, a nurse I didn't authorize, and you are both back here fucking while patients are lining the waiting room. I think that's more than reason enough."

Dr. Saas puffed up his chest. Oh, he was older than Hassan, but that didn't mean Hassan was going to let him off the hook. It was no wonder the people weren't coming to the clinic if this was what was going on.

"You're a young man, you don't have the balls for handling the clinics and the hospital. Go back and play at being a doctor."

Hassan barely kept his temper in check. "Another mistake." He turned and opened the door. His bodyguards stood there, and the rest of the hallway was empty. Good. Leaving the door open, Hassan marched to Dr. Saas and grabbed him by the collar. "I have the authority as minister of health, and you're done here." He dragged the man out of the room and pushed him to the back door.

Dr. Saas sputtered as the woman came scurrying out after them. Once they were both outside, Hassan closed the door and locked it. So much for him and Sara having a nice day together.

He glanced at his bodyguards. "Gentlemen, we have work to do." They nodded and walked back to the waiting room. Hassan fought to push his temper aside. The receptionist desk was empty, and Sara was quietly talking with people. He walked further into the room and several people looked up.

"Please accept my humble apologies for this mess. There is no reason for you to be sitting here waiting. Sara and I will start taking care of you just as fast as we can. Please give us a few minutes to get up to speed."

A chorus of "yes" and "of course" reached his ears. Sara

walked up to him. "Can your bodyguards please go get some food and water for them?" she asked softly. "Many of them have been waiting hours and were afraid to leave and lose their spot."

Hassan nodded, and his two bodyguards left. Najah stood near the entrance, and Hassan noticed the woman he'd been holding was now sitting in a chair. He ran his hand through his hair. "I'm going to call the hospital and see if they can send out another doctor and nurse." He touched Sara's cheek. "This wasn't how I expected us to spend our day."

Her lips turned up. "They are your people and need help. We can provide it, and I don't mind."

"Later, I'll make this up to you."

"You bet you will." She grinned before walking back across the room.

Later in the afternoon, Hassan scrubbed a hand down his face. Sara had been a godsend today. Not only had she catalogued everyone's ailments, but she prioritized them and was able to ascertain how long they'd been waiting.

She helped him with patients and when help from the hospital arrived, they'd been able to move people through quickly. Most of them had been simple cases, but it became obvious that Dr. Saas had been ignoring the patients for a while. Plus supplies and clinical equipment were missing.

They discovered this when Herma needed an X-ray and no one could find the machine. Hassan arranged to have her transported to the hospital, but she didn't want to go. She finally agreed to go if Sara accompanied her. An hour after Herma and Sara left, another group of volunteers descended on the clinic with supplies and smiles.

He looked around the empty waiting room with a sense of pride. They'd done it. Everyone had been seen or sent to the hospital for further help. But now he would have to find someone to cover the clinic. Today had shown him how much they needed more clinics and competent staff.

"I've finished taking inventory, Dr. Hassan," Jasmine said. She was one of the nurses who had come from the hospital to help.

"Thank you, Jasmine." While Sara had sent supplies, they still needed to restock.

"If you need, I don't mind working here at the clinic."

Hassan stared down at Jasmine. She was one of the newer nurses. "You don't want to be at the hospital?"

"It's not that," she said quickly. "I studied elder care. So many of our patients today were the older generation. I want to help them."

"I didn't know you'd studied elder care." What else didn't he know? He wanted people to be happy in their jobs. Feelings of failure swept through him. Maybe it was time for him to reevaluate his job. At first he had been able to juggle being a doctor and minster of health, but now ... too many things were slipping by.

"I didn't expect you to know. You're a good doctor. Our people trust you, I saw that today."

He smiled at the young woman. "I accept your generous offer. Thank you, Jasmine."

"You're welcome. I want to make you proud."

His chest swelled with pride. That was unexpected. "I don't know what to say."

"You don't have to say anything."

"I'll lock up." He found a spare set of keys and handed them to her. "The clinic is open nine to five, and I'll make sure your duty assignment is changed. I'm not sure who the doctor will be tomorrow. But Dr. Saas is not allowed on the premises. If he returns, please call the police and the hospital."

"I can do that."

"Good. Go home."

Hassan pulled the door closed behind him and glanced up at his bodyguards. "Let's go get Sara."

Hassan nodded to Najah from where he stood outside Sara's office at the hospital. He studied her as she worked. There were some lines of tiredness in her face. Her forehead wrinkled in concentration. "I didn't send you here to work even longer," he said.

Her head lifted, and her eyes lit up. "Hi. I just wanted to jot down some notes before I forgot them." She pushed her chair back, stood, and stretched.

Her breasts strained against the top she was wearing, and his cock jumped in response. He pushed his reaction to her down. The last thing he needed was to walk through the hospital and sit through dinner with a hard-on.

"Do you feel up to having dinner out tonight?"

"What do you have in mind?" She sashayed up to him.

His hands framed her waist. "I happen to know a little place not too far from here." He lowered his head. "Low lighting, private table, and fantastic food."

"You had me at dinner. I'm starving."

He frowned. "You shouldn't skip meals. Didn't you grab some lunch? I specifically told Najah to make sure you ate."

"I grabbed a power bar. That's all there was time for. Tell me, did you stop for lunch?"

He shook his head. He couldn't argue with her logic, nor deny he'd only eaten a power bar as well. But he didn't have to like it. Hassan guided her out of her office with the bodyguards following.

The night air was crisp, and he detected the sweet scents of jasmine and honey. "It's not far, are you okay to walk?"

"Yes." He enjoyed having her close to his side. Once they arrived, she noted that the building was pretty nondescript.

Hassan stopped and pushed the curtain around the

doorway back, gesturing for Sara to enter. She stepped inside, and he followed after gesturing for the bodyguards to wait outside.

The alcove lighting was dim. There was a woman seated near a second set of red curtains. She stood.

"Prince Hassan, welcome to you and your lady. Follow me, please," the woman said.

Sara jolted when the woman said Prince Hassan. So many called him Dr. Hassan, she often forgot he was royalty. He was also the most down-to-earth person she'd ever met.

The woman parted the curtains, and they walked through. Sara's breath caught in her throat. The room was lit by fixtures on the wall. They looked like ancient lamps. There were low tables in front of a small stage, with colorful pillows scatted around. Scents of meat, saffron, and other spices made her mouth water.

"This way, please," the woman said, leading them past several high-backed booths to an empty one in the corner. "Please enjoy your meal."

"Thank you," Hassan said. He gestured for Sara to slide into the booth. She did and he grinned. "All the way around to the back." She followed his instructions, and he slid in until his thigh touched hers.

"This is amazing." A beautiful glass chandelier hung from the ceiling. She ran her fingers over the fine lace tablecloth.

"Wafi's is one of our best restaurants."

"More than just a restaurant." She gestured toward the stage.

"Sometimes." His lips brushed her ear. "We might see some entertainment later, that is, if I don't sweep you back to my room and have my wicked way with you."

Her blood heated as a man stepped up to their table. "Prince Hassan and Lady Sara, I'm so humbled to have you grace my establishment tonight." He was dressed in a white caftan, his dark eyes dancing with joy. "If you need anything at all, please don't hesitate to let me know. In the meantime," he said, and snapped his fingers; water glasses were set on the table, along with little bowls of water and small hand towels, "please refresh yourselves. Would you like wine tonight?"

"Thank you, Wafi," Hassan said. "No wine tonight, but some of your refreshing fruit juice would be more than welcome."

"I'll have it sent over right away." He scurried off with the wait staff.

Sara stared at the items on the table. She had an idea of what to do, but she wasn't completely sure. She looked at Hassan.

A smile played around his lips. "Dip your fingers in the bowl, then dry them with the towel." He demonstrated, and she followed his lead. Once she was done, he moved the bowls and the towels off to the side.

A waiter approached the table. He set a platter of cheese,

fruit, and nuts in front of them, along with a pitcher of a yellow-colored liquid and glasses.

Sara's mouth watered. The power bar had been a long time ago. She glanced at the table once again. There were no plates or utensils. She looked at Hassan.

He had a mischievous glint in his eyes as if he knew what she was thinking. "I choose Wafi's for a reason." He reached over with his right hand, scooped up a piece of melon, and held it to her lips.

She opened her mouth and bit down on the melon. The sweet taste of honeydew exploded on her tongue. Hassan let out a groan before popping the rest of the melon in his mouth.

"Feeding you from my hand is one of the reasons." He nudged her thigh with his. "The second, I can sit close to you without worrying about prying eyes, and the third will come later." He washed his fingers in the bowl and dried them off.

A new waiter stopped at the table and set down two plates, one with pita bread and the other with something that looked like meatballs, before leaving once again.

"Falafel balls," Hassan said, picking up one of the small balls and holding it to her mouth. Sara opened her lips, and he popped the ball in.

She chewed and let out a moan as cumin, coriander, and garlic exploded on her tongue. "The spices are fantastic," she said after swallowing.

"We like our spices, but you'll find the combinations

pleasing to the taste buds." He popped one of the falafel balls into his mouth before pouring the yellow-colored beverage into a tall glass.

"Why no plates or utensils?" she asked out of curiosity. While they ate family-style at the palace, there were always plates and utensils.

"We are eating old-style. In this case, old-style means we use our fingers or scoop up food with pita bread."

"Oh." She reached for a piece of bread, and Hassan slapped her fingers.

"No, sweetheart." He grasped her fingers and brought them to his lips, kissing where he had playfully hit her. "Tonight, I feed you."

Sara tilted her head and studied Hassan. He was serious. She'd never had a man feed her before. "I thought you were only doing it for fun."

"Fun and pleasure." He released her hand. "It pleases me to feed you, but also, I love watching the expression on your face as you eat."

Her cheeks grew warm. This was why she couldn't play poker or lie well. Her face always gave her away. She tucked her chin down.

"Hey." Warm fingers lifted her chin until their gazes locked. "No being embarrassed or afraid. I'm the luckiest man in this room to be with you tonight."

"But ... " He trailed his thumb over her lips, stopping her words.

"I want to feed you, to take care of you tonight. Will you let me?"

Her bones melted at his husky voice. When was the last time she'd let someone take care of her this way? Never. She'd never trusted anyone enough, but with Hassan the trust was there. She nodded and he relaxed, removing his fingers from her lips.

"Thank you. I will honor your trust in me."

His words hit her low in the stomach, making not only her body heat with desire, but her mind accept a newfound knowledge of Hassan's personality. The waiter arrived and set two steaming bowls of lamb stew on the table.

She sat back and waited. Hassan scooped up some stew with the bread and held it to her lips. She took the tasty morsel. That was how dinner continued. The fruit juice was tangy but refreshing.

By the time dessert was brought out, Sara didn't think she could take another bite.

"Halvah," Hassan said as it was set on the table.

"It looks like cake, but yet different."

"It is." He picked up a spoon and scooped up a bit and held it to her lips. "Trust me."

Sara parted her lips, and her eyes closed in bliss when the confection burst flavors over her taste buds. "Oh, my goodness," she said after she swallowed. "This is heaven."

"Halvah is made from ground sesame seeds and sugar. I'm not sure what this one is flavored with."

"Pistachio." She identified it easily. "It's different and good."

Hassan took a bite and then grinned. "It is, almost as sweet as you are."

She let out a laugh. "You're flirting with me."

"I want to do more than flirt."

Sara shifted. Heat flooded her body. She wanted to do so much more than flirt as well, but they were in public. But she could be discrete. She slid her hand over to Hassan's lap.

"Sara?" His voice dropped.

She tilted her head and nodded toward the dessert. "More, please."

He scooped up another bite of halvah and fed it to her. She traced his cock with her fingers, and it bulged against his slacks. Hassan stiffened and she paused.

"Don't stop." His voice was hushed.

His words empowered her. She continued to caress him through his trousers, and he kept feeding her halvah until it was gone. The lights dimmed, and she glanced at him.

"Entertainment." His voice was strained.

Sara hid a smile. Her fingers found the button on his pants. She worked it loose before lowering the zipper.

"Sara." His voice was low, but he shifted closer to her.

"Let me do this for you." She'd never done anything like this in public before. While she'd been flogged at the club in London, she always had on a thong, but she'd never played with her Dom.

Now she wanted to please Hassan, to give him pleasure that didn't involve food. She pushed his underwear out of the way, and his cock sprang free. It was hard and hot against her skin. She inhaled and took him in her hand. His soft groan and the shifting of his hips let her know he was on board with this.

Music began to play, a low, soulful beat that matched the thumping of her pulse. She lay her head on his shoulder while her hand traced him from base to head and back again.

"So hard, hot, and mine," she murmured, enjoying the feel of him against her skin. The knowledge that she was making him this way was more intoxicating than alcohol.

His cock jumped. "Ah, he's eager." She kept her voice low. "Yes, he is."

Her lips twitched. "Good. I love the feel of him in my hand." Her nail traced one of the pulsing veins.

Hassan's eyes closed and his hips shifted. "You're playing with fire." His fingers curled into his palms where they rested on the table.

"Maybe I want to get burned."

She kept her gaze on his face. His lashes rose, and his blue eyes flared with hot, burning passion. He shifted toward her, and his left hand rose and gripped the back of her neck before his lips descended.

He took what he wanted. His tongue thrust into her mouth as she stroked his dick. Little shudders racked his body. She'd never felt so powerful, and yet so dominated by a kiss.

Their tongues tangled and chased each other around until he broke the kiss. "Stop," he said against her lips. She stilled her hand. "As much as I want you to keep touching me, we're in public, and a few more strokes and I'm going to go off like a rocket."

"And that's a bad thing?" She punctuated each word with a brush of her lips against his, tasting their dessert.

"My coming from your wonderful touch, no. In public, yes."

"I could take you in my mouth. No mess then." Where was this coming from? Even with all her experience as a submissive, she'd never offered to take a man in her mouth before. But the idea of doing it with Hassan sent hot tendrils of fire through her blood.

His fingers tightened on the back of her neck. "No, my sweetness." His voice was strained. "When you take me in your mouth, I want to be able to watch you."

The tension in his face told her everything she needed to know. He was close to breaking, and she wouldn't push him over. Not tonight. "Very well, shall I tuck you back in and zip you up?" She fought to keep the disappointment out of her voice. But they could play later, in private.

"Let me do it."

Sara released his cock, and he let go of her neck. She put several inches between their bodies. Their gazes locked. He tucked his dick away, and another shudder swept through his body. He grasped her hand. "Let's get out of here." He slid out of the booth and helped Sara to her feet.

"Everything okay?" Wafi asked when they neared the door.

"Perfect, Wafi," Hassan said. "We ... " He glanced at her, passion still glowing in his eyes.

"Ah, young love. Go enjoy the evening, my friend."

Hassan nodded. He pushed the curtains aside, and with Sara close to his side, they walked outside. Camera flashes blinded her when they stepped out the door.

"Damn it," he said under his breath. He drew her closer to his side.

Najah and the other two bodyguards were there, clearing a path to a car. "I called when they arrived," Najah said.

"Prince Hassan, are you and Ms. Fairchild an item?" a reporter yelled.

"Why did you go to Wafi's tonight?" another voice yelled.

"Do you have anything to say about the unlawful firing of Dr. Saas from the clinic today?"

Hassan stiffened. While she was aware he'd fired the neglectful doctor, what right did they have to question him? She lifted her head to chew out the reporter, but Hassan placed his palm against the side of her face, keeping her tucked close to his chest.

Ignoring the shouting reporters and the cameras going off, he continued to make his way to the car. Najah held the door open and they climbed in. Then Najah followed, shutting the door behind him. The other two bodyguards slid into the front seat.

"How long were they outside, Najah?" He pulled on his safety belt and made sure Sara's was done up before the car pulled away.

"They showed up right after you and Lady Sara went inside."

"Thank you for calling for a car." Hassan turned to her. "Are you okay?"

"Fine. Why did they show up at Wafi's?" Her brow creased. "Do you think it's a coincidence they mentioned Dr. Saas?"

"I'm not sure why they showed up, but we'll find out when we get back to the palace."

Malik and his father were waiting for them when the car pulled up, their faces grim.

"This does not look good," Sara muttered.

"Go upstairs. I'll come by your room if it's not too late." He led her up the stairs to where his family waited.

Sara hesitated, then shook her head. "No. If this has something to do with what happened at the clinic, I was there. They might want my opinion."

Hassan's gaze went from her to his brother and father.

"I, for one, would like Sara's opinion," Malik said.

Hassan nodded, and they followed Malik and his father into Malik's office. Sara stifled a sigh. They were spending a lot of time in this office. Once they were seated, Malik handed Hassan a newspaper.

Sara glanced at the headline when Hassan held it up. "Is Prince Hassan neglecting his job? Is he fit to stay health minister?"

"What a load of shit." The words were out of her mouth before she could censor them. She slapped her hand over her mouth.

Hassan's jaw dropped at Sara's words. He'd never heard her swear before. He hid his grin behind his hand.

"Damn, I like you," Malik said with smile.

"You said what we were all thinking." His father patted her arm since he was seated next to her.

"Tomorrow's paper?" Hassan tossed the offending story on Malik's desk. The press was making the family's life hell.

"I'm afraid so," Malik said. "What do we do?"

"It's not true," Sara burst out. "You can't believe what they're printing."

Pride swelled in Hassan's body at Sara's defense of him. She didn't even question the paper's account, but championed him, even if his family hadn't asked her to.

"Sara," Malik started. "We never said we believed the paper."

"Actually," Jamal said, "Hassan is well within his rights to fire Dr. Saas. The problem is, Dr. Saas is saying Hassan fired him for no cause."

Hassan shifted in his seat, but before he could say anything, Sara jumped into the fire.

"But Dr. Saas was having sex with his nurse while patients waited." Sara groaned. "I can't keep my mouth shut tonight."

Hassan patted her hand. "I would have told them the same thing."

His brother looked shell-shocked, and his father was shaking his head. "He was ... " Jamal started, but then closed his mouth.

"Well, that certainly puts a spin on things," Malik said, sitting back in his chair. "You and Sara were scheduled to visit the clinic today?"

"Yes, but I didn't exactly announce it. It was going to be a quick visit so she could get an idea of what our clinics are like."

"I was talking to a local woman who had fallen a few days ago. I had Najah carry her to the clinic. That's when I saw the waiting room was full and the receptionist didn't have clue, so I went back to get Hassan," Sara told them.

"Without Najah?" Malik frowned.

"Yes." She lifted her chin, and Hassan fought against cheering. She wasn't going to be a pushover for anyone. "I can take care of myself, but that's beside the point. I got Hassan, and together we went back to the clinic."

"I was appalled by what I saw," Hassan said. "I'm the one

insisting on having the clinics, and the one in my own city was a mess." Part of him was upset he hadn't paid more attention to the clinic. He knew how important this outreach was to his people.

"I agreed with your decision about the clinics and hiring Dr. Saas," Jamal said.

Hassan nodded. "Sara and I went to find the doctor. There was a closed exam room door. I knocked, then opened the door. He was engaged in relations with his nurse on the exam table."

"Engaged in relations? That's a nice euphemism," Malik commented.

Hassan shook his head. "I sent Sara back to the waiting room. I told Saas to pull up his pants and get the hell out of the clinic, and both he and the nurse were fired. He argued with me, so I pushed him out the back door. My two new bodyguards were there and witnessed everything."

"That's a plus," Malik said, laying his hands on his desk.

"While Hassan was dealing with the doctor, I started gathering names, ailments, and other information from the people waiting. We have documentation. When his two bodyguards came out, I sent them to get food and water because too many people had been waiting all day to be seen," Sara added.

Malik frowned. "Isn't the clinic supposed to be stocked with water, at a minimum?"

"Another issue." Hassan ran his hand over his face. "Not

only did I find no water or snacks, half the supplies are missing, along with the X-ray machine."

Malik swore. "It looks like Dr. Saas has been financing his own little world. What is the plan?"

"Supplies were delivered. I've ordered another X-ray machine." He glanced at Sara. "Fazil isn't going to be happy about the expenditure."

"Leave him to me," Sara said, folding her hands in her lap. Her voice was firm.

Jamal laughed. "You remind me of my Anna and Catherine. Soft on the outside, but a spine of steel."

"I'll take that as a compliment." Sara smiled at Jamal, but Hassan was thinking that his father was right, Sara was a strong woman.

"We've got the full story. Here's what I propose." Malik leaned forward, elbows on his desk. "Hassan, you and Sara will be part of a press conference tomorrow morning. You'll tell your side of the story. I have a feeling once word gets out, several people will come forward and corroborate it."

"I'd rather not involve Sara," Hassan said. He didn't want her to be subject to the press. They were vultures, and he remembered how Catherine had reacted.

"It's fine." She took his hand in hers. "I don't mind, and everyone needs to know you were doing your job."

"The press will want to know more than about the clinic. They found you both at Wafi's tonight," Jamal said.

Sara's eyes widened, then she shook her head. "So we're

attracted to each other. It was just dinner to get to know each other better."

Hassan's blood heated at her words. Good; he wanted more than just someone to dominate in the bedroom, he wanted a partner.

"Then we phrase it as such," Malik said. "You both get some sleep. The press conference is set for nine."

"You already set it up?" Hassan glared at his brother.

"Yes. You wouldn't have fired Dr. Saas without good reason, I just didn't know why until now."

Hassan stood, pulling Sara to her feet. "Meddling brother." He led Sara from the room. "You do realize the press is going to eat you up tomorrow," he said as they climbed the stairs to their rooms.

"I can handle them." She stopped outside her room. "Are you coming in?"

"I want to." Her hopeful expression gave him strength. "But we're going to have an early morning."

"But ... " A noise from inside her room made her frown.

Hassan put his fingers to his lips. He turned his head and motioned to Najah. Within a minute, Najah and another guard stood next to him. Hassan quietly told him what they'd heard.

"Stay out here," Najah said, giving him a pointed look.

Hassan nodded and pulled Sara off to the side. "Hassan?" Her eyes were wide.

"Shhhh." He cradled her against his body. She trembled against him.

The sound of a scuffle, breaking glass, and then a shout had them both tensing up.

"Can you see what is going on?" she asked in a soft voice.

"No. We will stay here until Najah tells us everything is okay."

Another shout came from the room, and the guard ran out and bolted down the stairs. This was not good. Keeping Sara close, Hassan guided them down the hall to Malik's and Catherine's room. He knocked and within seconds the door opened to a concerned Catherine.

"What's going on?" she asked.

"Keep Sara with you, and make sure all the windows and doors are locked. Do not open your door to anyone but me, Malik, Samir, or Najah." Hassan pushed Sara into the room when Catherine held the door open. He then pulled the door shut and waited until the lock was thrown before sprinting back down the hallway to Sara's room. He stopped inside the doorway. The room was a mess.

The table had been knocked over, the vase was broken, water soaked the carpet, and flowers had been trampled. The balcony doors were wide open. Hassan frowned. Sara never would have left the doors unlocked, let alone open.

He made his way carefully to the balcony, making sure not to touch or step on anything. He glanced over the railing. Najah and other guards were searching the grounds.

"Najah," he called.

"Hassan, go back inside. I'll send a guard up to check your room," Khalid yelled, frustration in his voice.

"All right." Hassan retraced his steps and stepped into the hall. A guard approached him, along with Malik.

"What the hell is going on?" Malik asked.

"Please, sir," the guard said.

Malik shook his head and looked at Hassan, who said, "I think someone broke into Sara's room. She is with Catherine in your rooms. As soon as the guard checks my room, I'll get Sara. Khalid and the guards are searching the grounds."

Malik nodded, turned, and marched down the hall. He knocked on the door and waited. "It's me, sweetheart. It's okay to open the door."

Hassan kept his gaze on Malik until he was safely in his room, then he looked at the guard.

"Prince Hassan, please wait out here while I check your room," the guard said, pushing open Hassan's door.

Hassan didn't like cooling his heels in the hallway, but what choice did he have? Someone had broken into Sara's room. The question was how and why. The guard reemerged and gestured to the open door.

"Your room is clear, sir. Please keep all the doors and windows locked. Sound the alarm if anything unusual happens."

"Of course. Let me get Sara. and then you can go." Hassan made his way to Malik's room and knocked.

"Yes." Malik's strong voice came through the door.

"It's me," Hassan said.

The door opened a sliver, then all the way. "You might as well come in. I think it would be better if we stayed together."

"I'm staying with Malik, please go help Khalid," Hassan told the guard before slipping into the room. Malik shut the door and locked it.

Catherine and Sara were huddled together on the sofa. Sara looked up at him and, with a small cry, she launched herself into his arms. "Why didn't you come in here with me?"

"I'm fine, sweetheart." Hassan rubbed his palms up and down Sara's back. He glanced over her shoulder at Malik, who was hugging Catherine close.

"What is going on?" Catherine asked. "I heard the breaking of glass and then running feet."

Malik's features tightened. "Did you hear anything before that?" He sat down in an overstuffed chair and pulled Catherine into his lap.

Catherine shook her head.

Sara looked up at him, her eyes wide. "Someone broke into my room?"

"It looks like that."

"It never should have happened. Where were the guards? Security was tightened since Catherine snuck out." Malik drew a hand through his hair, clearly frustrated.

"We'll have to wait for Najah and Samir's report, but I

guarantee you Khalid is not happy." He remembered the frustration in their brother's voice. "Where is Rafi? And our parents?"

"Rafi is out at the stables. Mom and Dad are in their room with their bodyguards."

Hassan guided Sara over to the sofa and gestured for her to sit. When she did, he sat down beside her.

"I thought they fixed the gap in the fence I used to slip through," Catherine said, laying her head on Malik's shoulder.

"They did."

Sara looked up at Hassan, and Hassan slipped his arm around her shoulders, pulling her close. It was going to be a long night.

Sara snuggled close to Hassan and waited. Why would someone break into her room? She never left the doors unlocked. Hassan was tense, and so was Malik. She couldn't blame them.

Her gaze met Catherine's, and Catherine shrugged. There wasn't much they could do until someone told them what was going on.

A knock on the door made them all jump. Malik stood with Catherine in his arms before setting her on her feet. Hassan stood and motioned Catherine to the sofa, then took up a position between the women and the door.

Malik opened the door and Samir, Catherine's bodyguard, stepped in. Malik closed the door but didn't lock it, so Sara figured the danger was past.

"Crown Princess Catherine, Lady Sara, Prince Hassan, and my king," Samir said with a slight bow.

"Dispense with the formalities, Samir. Tell us what happened," Malik said.

Samir glanced at Sara and Catherine, and Sara hid a smile. The men were always trying to protect them. In a way it was charming, in another annoying.

"Someone broke into Lady Sara's room."

"That much we figured out," Hassan muttered.

"We chased him and ... " Again Samir's gaze settled on Sara and Catherine.

"Please tell us, Samir," Catherine said.

"We cornered him. Before we could question him, he took his own life."

Catherine let out a little cry, and Sara took her hand. "It's okay, Catherine." Catherine hated the thought of anyone taking their own life.

"Any idea of who he was?" Hassan asked, as Malik took Catherine into his arms to comfort her.

"Yes. It was one of Kalif's men."

Sara frowned. "This doesn't make sense," she said. "Why break into my room?"

Samir raised his hands in the air and then let them drop. "We don't know. He could have been looking for Hassan's room, or even Malik's. We just don't know."

"I want to know how he got on the grounds, let alone into Sara's room, without being seen," Malik said.

"Prince Khalid is on that right now, sir. We will have answers, but probably not until morning."

Malik let out a breath. "Understood. Thank you, Samir."

Samir left the room, and Sara turned her attention to Hassan, who was watching her.

"I'm not leaving you alone tonight," he told her.

"Hassan, this isn't the place to discuss it." She closed her eyes for a moment, then opened them.

"Actually, it's perfect," Malik said.

"Malik, let them have some privacy," Catherine said.

"My room?" Hassan asked.

Sara nodded, rose to her feet, and padded over to where Catherine and Malik stood. "I'm fine. Don't worry." She kissed her friend on the cheek before turning to Hassan.

"Tomorrow," he said to Malik, then, taking her by the arm, led her from Malik's room and down the hall to his room. Inside his room, he locked the main door and checked the balcony doors.

Hassan crossed back to her and pulled her into a tight embrace. A small shudder ran through his body. "Hassan?" she asked.

"What if we hadn't heard the noise before you entered

your room? What if you'd walked in there, alone?"

The fear in his voice tugged at her heart. She'd thought about the same thing. "It didn't happen, and we can't dwell on what-ifs." She had tried to do that once before. Her past wasn't sparkly clean, but going over and over her mistakes only made things worse. She'd learned from her mistakes and moved on.

His arms tightened even more. She put her arms around his waist and held him. He needed some reassurance. He was worried about what had happened, and he was worried about her well-being. This strong man had a very tender and protective side. Outside of Catherine, it had been a long time since anyone had really worried or cared about her.

They stood there until Hassan pulled back and stared down at her. "You're sleeping here tonight. In my bed, in my arms, where I know you're safe."

She opened her mouth to argue, but the fear in his blue eyes made her rethink. He needed reassurance she was safe, and staying with him would help. "All right. We should probably try and get some sleep. It's after midnight, and the press conference will be here before we know it."

"By all means, my lady." He swept his arm out in front of him, and Sara's mood lightened.

Hassan lay awake watching Sara sleep. He couldn't stop

thinking about what might have happened if she'd walked into her room tonight. Would he have been able to save her? Would he even have known something was wrong? What did Kalif want with Sara?

He couldn't answer a single question, and he hated it. But he could keep Sara close, and he intended to. He wasn't going to lose her. She'd argue with him, and he was okay with that. He liked the way she stood up for herself and her beliefs.

He'd watched her today as they walked through town toward the clinic. She had stopped and talked to people. Guilt crept into him. She'd come to visit Catherine, yet here she was helping him with the clinics. Her ideas were great, and the business plan she had drawn up was spot on.

Sara shifted in her sleep, and he tightened his arms around her. He'd given her one of his T-shirts to sleep in. He glanced at the clock. It was after three in the morning. He needed to rest. The press conference was going to be interesting tomorrow, especially after tonight's events. He needed to be on his A game.

"I'm to wear that?" Sara gestured to the intricately designed caftan lying across the sofa in Catherine's room. Hassan had refused to let her return to her room; he sent a maid in to get her clean underwear, her toothbrush, and some clothes. She was touched by his overprotectiveness.

"Yes." Catherine put her hands on her hips. "We don't have much time, since you and Hassan both overslept. Anything I should know about?" Catherine gave a sly smile.

Sara laughed, but her cheeks grew warm. "We slept together, no sex, no anything. Actually, I slept the most. Hassan was awake for half the night."

"If you were asleep, then how do you know he was awake?"

"Because he told me," Sara said, as Catherine pushed her toward the bedroom.

"With everything that's been going on, we haven't had a chance to really talk," Catherine said, laying the garment on the bed.

"I know." Sara let out a sigh. "Some friend I am. I come to visit, and instead I take on a job."

Catherine shook her head. "It's fine. You're doing something you love, and I don't mind. You'd be bored without something to occupy you. I want to warn you, the press is going to make a big deal out of what happened." Catherine gestured with her hands.

"At the clinic or the break-in last night?"

"Probably both. Come sit down, and I'll do your makeup." Catherine patted the small stool in front of the vanity table.

"Shouldn't I put the caftan on first?" Catherine shook her head and Sara sat down. "Not too much makeup."

"Just enough to highlight your eyes." Catherine opened

MARIE TUHART

several items on the vanity. "So, tell me, have you and Hassan made love yet?"

"Catherine!" Sara pretended to be outraged, but she and Catherine shared everything. "I've only been here a little over a week. We haven't had much time for anything."

"Close your eyes."

Sara did as Catherine said. "We discussed playing together, then the stuff with the clinic came up yesterday. I think Hassan planned on playing last night but with what happened ... " She shrugged her shoulders.

"Malik was hands-on last night."

"Oh, my, do you think Hassan and Malik talk to each other like we do?" Her stomach turned over. She wasn't sure if she was ready for Malik to know all her secrets.

"Malik is closemouthed at times. If they do, don't worry. Malik won't say anything." A snap reached Sara's ears. "Open your eyes and tell me what you think."

Sara opened her eyes, and her hand fluttered to her chest. Catherine had used gold and green to highlight her eyes. A little bit of blush gave more color to her cheeks. "It's perfect."

"Good. Now stand up and strip to your undies, girl."

"Do I really have to go that far?" Sara removed her slacks and blouse.

"Yes, trust me on this. Everything will be okay." Catherine picked up the garment and slipped it over Sara's head, making sure to keep the fabric away from her face.

The fabric caressed Sara's skin as it slid down. It was silky smooth, but not slippery. She'd never felt fabric like this.

"Perfect. I was hoping I got your size right. You'd think after our living together I'd know your size."

Sara looked at her friend. "What do you mean?"

"I had one of the local seamstresses make this for you."

"But why?" Sara tilted her head. What was her friend up to?

"Because you need something that makes you feel feminine but also shows you off to the people of Bashir."

"And this will do it?" Sara glanced at herself in the mirror. The caftan didn't cling to her body, yet it enhanced her curves.

"Yes. We need shoes." Catherine rummaged around in her closet and emerged with a pair of shoes.

They looked like ballet flats, but they were decorated with beads and shiny fake jewels. Catherine knelt down and slipped them on Sara's feet. "Perfect. Go look in the full length mirror."

Sara walked over and stopped. Was that really her? In the vanity mirror she'd only seen her top half, but the full-length version ... The colors in the caftan brought out her blonde hair and made her skin look tan. "This is beautiful. You're a miracle worker."

"No miracles." Catherine smiled. "Come on, we better get going, or we'll be late." Catherine took Sara's hand and tugged her out of the room.

Hassan paced around the main reception room. He hated press conferences. Normally they were left to Malik, but on occasion, for the hospital, he had to make them. He was worried about this one. In the last twenty-four hours so much had happened.

"Nervous?" Malik asked.

"A bit." Hassan smoothed his hands over his robe. Usually he didn't bother with his royal formal wear, but this morning Malik had asked him to please wear it.

"Why are you insisting Sara be at this press conference?" He had tried again this morning to keep her out of it, but Malik insisted.

"Because she saw what happened. Plus this affects her as well. She's impartial; well, as impartial as you can get being friends with the soon-to-be new queen and one of the princes."

"Where are our parents? I thought they'd both be here."

Malik ran a hand over his face. "Khalid sent them to the summer palace, thinking it would be safer until we figure out what is going on."

"Good idea." He was sure his father had protested the entire time, but he was glad their parents were out of the line of fire. "How are the wedding plans coming along?" Malik had to be going nuts with running the country, dealing with everything that was happening, and trying to plan his wedding.

"If I had my way, we'd get on a plane and get married in England."

"And deprive the people of Bashir of a royal wedding."

Malik laughed, and it helped Hassan relax. "Just wait." Malik clapped him on the shoulder. "Your time will come, and I'll have the last laugh."

Hassan opened his mouth to reply, but lost his words as Sara and Catherine walked into the room. Sara was dressed in a beautifully woven caftan filled with the royal colors. Her green eyes were bright, and she had a shy smile on her lips. He guessed Catherine had Sara put the gown on, and he'd bet his career Sara had no idea what the colors meant. Oh, this was going to be a fun press conference.

"We're wearing the same colors," Sara said, and Hassan hid a smile. Today had just gotten more interesting.

"Yes, we are." He took her hand in his.

Malik smirked, and Catherine just smiled.

"Five minutes," Khalid said. Hassan noticed that his brother looked tired.

"Any news?" he asked. Khalid had been up all night trying to find out how the man had gotten in and to see if they could find out why Sara had been the target.

"Not really. We can't figure out how he got in, but I will figure it out."

"You need to rest," Hassan said, worried his brother was

burning the candle at both ends. After their father's heart attack, Hassan was keeping a closer eye on everyone's health.

"I will." Khalid inclined his head. "Once I make sure the family is safe."

Malik stepped up to the pair. "Hassan is right. After the press conference is over, I want you to go get some sleep." Khalid opened his mouth, but Malik interrupted. "Don't make me pull rank."

"Bossy brother," Khalid muttered.

"Yes, he is," Hassan said with a smile.

The door opened. Samir and Najah strode in. "Everyone is assembled and ready," Najah said.

"Were there any complaints?" Khalid asked.

"A little grumbling," Samir said.

"Complaints about what?" Sara asked.

Khalid turned his gaze to her. "We had the members of the press searched before they could step foot on the palace grounds."

"Oh." Worry crossed her features.

"Nothing to worry about, little sister," Khalid said. "It was just a precaution."

Hassan hid his surprise at Khalid calling Sara "little sister." His brother was already treating her as one of the family. "Where is Rafi?"

Khalid's features tightened. "He's insisting on staying down at the stables. Two of the mares are ready to give birth."

"He's protective of his horses," Malik said.

"I'd rather have him in the palace," Khalid muttered.

"His bodyguard is with him, correct?" Malik asked.

"Yes."

"Then let go of the worry, brother," Hassan said, clasping his brother's shoulder. "You know his bodyguard would die before he'd let Rafi get hurt."

Khalid nodded. "It's time."

Hassan's hand tightened around Sara's. "Nervous?" he asked.

"A little."

"It will be fine." He raised her hand to his lips and placed a soft kiss on her knuckles. Her green eyes brightened with desire. Maybe tonight they could spend some time together. He tucked her hand into the crook of his elbow and escorted her into the press room.

The room fell silent when they entered, then a low murmur started. Keeping Sara close, he guided her up onto the raised platform before stepping up to the podium.

"Thank you all for coming today." His gaze took in the room. There were at least forty people there; some he recognized and others he didn't. Why were so many interested in the story? "I understand Dr. Saas has been speaking to some of you about his side of the story."

Several hands shot up. Hassan pointed to the first one he saw.

"Thank you, Prince Hassan. Dr. Saas claims you fired him without cause, any comment?" the reporter asked.

"I fired Dr. Saas for an ethics violation." He fought to keep his temper in check.

"What did he do?" another reporter shouted.

"Dr. Saas ignored a waiting room full of patients, some who had been waiting hours to be seen, while he was in a back room with his nurse." That was an image he wished he could erase from his mind.

The murmurs grew louder. "Are you saying Dr. Saas was having sex with his nurse in the clinic?" another reported asked.

"Yes." He could only hope this didn't kill all chances they had to get the new clinics up and running.

"Ms. Fairchild, what were you doing at the clinic?"

Hassan glanced at Sara, who answered, "I asked Prince Hassan to show me the clinic. The prince would like to open more of them, and I agreed to help him as I have a background in medicine." Her voice was calm, and it helped soothe his nerves.

"Is it true Prince Hassan hit Dr. Saas?"

Hassan stiffened.

"Is that what he is saying?" Sara squeezed his arm.

"He mentioned it."

Hassan took a calming breath. "I did not hit him. I simply told Dr. Saas and the nurse to get dressed. Then I fired them both and escorted them out the back door of the clinic."

"And that was it?" The reporter was insistent.

"Yes. Ms. Fairchild and I began seeing patients and called the hospital for help."

Sara shifted beside him and she said in a low voice, "Tell them the rest."

"While we were helping the people, it was discovered that most of the supplies and the X-ray machine were missing."

The volume in the room increased. Stealing was not tolerated in Bashir. It was a fairly wealthy country. Health care was free, the prices of medicine were kept down to the bare cost, and the government worked to make sure every child was educated and able to decide his or her own future.

"What about the break-in at the palace last night?" a new reporter called out.

Hassan frowned. Khalid had warned him this could come up.

"That is all my fault." Sara gave a laugh. "I forgot to close my balcony doors when I left yesterday morning. Last night, when I walked into my room, the wind blew the curtain and it startled me." She grinned at the crowd. "I screamed."

"And?" a female reporter called out.

"Prince Hassan and half the guards came running."

"How did the vase get broken?" a reporter in the back asked.

Hassan glanced over at Najah and Samir. They nodded. There was no way any reporter should have known about the vase unless one of the palace guards had told him. Hassan opened his mouth to reply, but Sara beat him to it.

"The guards were in a rush, and they bumped the table where the vase was sitting. It was all a big misunderstanding. I'm happy to say the vase wasn't valuable, and I learned my lesson about leaving doors open."

A laugh went through the crowd. Hassan was so proud of Sara. She had deflected the reporter's questions and protected all of them at the same time.

"What about dinner at Wafi's last night?"

"That is private," Hassan said, his voice low and tight.

"Prince Hassan, nothing is private where the royal family is concerned," another reporter said.

Sara squeezed his arm again. He glanced at her.

"Please," Sara said. "I know you want a story, but you're barking up the wrong tree. Prince Hassan took me to Wafi's so I could experience the local culture."

"Why are you so interested in Bashir?" the woman reporter asked.

"How can I not be?" Sara waved her hand. "My best friend is marrying your new king, and I'll be visiting a lot. I want to understand the people and the culture. Wouldn't you?"

The room burst into laughter. "And the fact that you and Prince Hassan are wearing matching robes?" the woman asked.

"A happy accident," Sara said.

Khalid stepped forward. "This press conference is now over."

Questions were shouted as Hassan escorted Sara out of the room, with Samir, Najah, and Khalid following. Malik and Catherine were waiting for them. Khalid nodded at Mailk before leaving with Samir and Najah.

"Well done," Malik said.

Sara slumped down onto one of the chairs. "Holy crap, those reporters can be relentless."

"Told you," Catherine said, crossing to her friend and taking the chair next to her. "But you did fantastic."

"How they hell did they know about the vase?" Hassan's anger flared. "No one outside of the palace should know about that."

"I wondered about that too," Sara said.

"You covered it well," Malik said.

"Yeah, well, it was a spur-of-the-moment thing."

Hassan strode over to Sara and knelt. "I'm sorry about all this. It's my job to protect you."

"Hassan." She cupped his cheek. Her warm skin caressed his. "None of this is your fault."

"It is." He would take responsibility for his failures.

"No, it's not." Her voice was strong, and her gaze held his. "It happened, and we will deal with it. No one is at fault."

"Someone is," Malik muttered.

"Okay, however the guy got in, and whoever leaked to the

press about the incident. But that doesn't mean we have to confirm it."

Hassan's admiration for Sara lifted even higher.

"Damn, when did you learn all this?" Catherine asked.

Sara laughed. "I know how much you hate the press, and with everything that has happened in your life, I don't blame you. I, because of some of my nursing work, had to interact with them. I began studying them and what they did."

"Always learning," Catherine said softly.

"Yes. I have a question, though. What is the big deal about Hassan and me wearing matching robes?" Sara glanced at her friend, and Hassan hid a smile.

"Busted," Catherine said.

"What did you do, Catherine?"

"I just made sure the caftan you wore contained the royal colors." Catherine ducked her head.

"Catherine, you didn't tell her," Malik said.

"Hey, you did it to me." Catherine held up her hands as Malik approached. Hassan had to bite back a laugh. Yes, his brother had done that.

"That was to protect you." Malik drew her to her feet. "If we were alone ... " he teased.

Sara's cheeks bloomed, and Hassan's grin widened. She turned her attention to him. "Why are you smiling? You knew."

"Guilty." He wasn't going to deny it. "You look beautiful in the royal colors."

"It's only going to fuel more speculation," she said, letting her hand drop from his face.

"Let it." He really didn't care. Hassan was finding life with Sara fun and intriguing. Hopefully they could spend some time together today. With everything happening in the last twenty-four hours, he'd made sure someone could cover for him at the hospital. It was time to explore this relationship.

"But what about your parents?" She kept her voice low.

"They will be happy for us."

"But," Sara said, and shook her head, "I ... "

Hassan placed his fingers over her lips and pulled her to her feet. "Are you ready for some us time?" he asked low enough that only she would hear him.

Sara blinked at him, her green eyes bright.

"If you'll excuse us," Malik said. Hassan glanced at his brother to see Malik holding Catherine in his arms. "It's time for me to discipline my soon-to-be wife and queen."

"Malik!" The outrage in Catherine's voice made Hassan laugh as Malik swung her up into his arms and strode out of the room.

"They are good for each other," Sara said.

"We can be too." Was she still worried about them?

"We haven't even played yet."

"Then by all means, let's play today." He slipped his arm around her waist.

"Don't you have to get to the hospital?"

"No." He guided her from the room. "I have the day off,

and I'm going to devote it to you."

She trembled in his hold, but her eyes were bright with desire. "Then by all means, let's play."

Fire spread through Hassan's body. "I want you to go to your room, take a shower, and prepare your body. In thirty minutes, come to my room in nothing but your robe."

"Just my robe?"

"That is correct."

"Yes ... Sir."

"Go." They'd reached the top of the stairs and stood outside Sara's door. He nodded at the guard, who turned and marched away. Hassan turned the knob and pushed the door open. "Thirty minutes. If you are late I will punish you." With those words, he nudged her into her room and then walked to his. He had a lot to do in thirty minutes.

Sara could barely contain herself. Excitement and anticipation flowed through her body. Even with everything that had happened in the last twenty-four hours, she couldn't wait to play with Hassan.

After her shower, she dried off and slipped on her robe and a pair of slippers. Sara turned and unpinned her hair and brushed it out. Her eyes were bright and her nipples hard.

It had been too long since she played. She glanced at her

watch sitting on the counter. Three minutes. She'd better get a move on. She moved across her suite and to the door, opening it and looking out. Good—no one in the hallway.

She hurried down the hall to Hassan's room and knocked. The door opened, and she stepped inside. Her breath caught in her throat as the door snicked shut behind her.

Hassan had pushed all the furniture in the sitting room to the edge, and in the middle of the room stood a multiuse table. There were candles around the room, making the room glow in the low light.

"Someone has been busy."

"Yes." His hand cupped her elbow. "Come sit down." He led her over to a small table for two. Two tapers were lit, and plates were covered. Hassan held out her chair and she sat, being careful not to let the robe fall open.

He paused behind her with his hands on her shoulders. "You didn't eat breakfast."

"No." She swallowed. She'd been too nervous to think about food. Her stomach turned over.

"First we will eat, and talk, then play." He lifted the lid off the plate. The scent of the bacon next to the eggs on the plate tickled her nose.

Hassan took his seat across from her. Sara lifted her fork and began to eat. This wasn't the first time she'd eaten in a robe, but it was the first time she'd eaten with Hassan alone in his room.

Her stomach fluttered. She wanted this, so much. To explore this attraction she had to him, but also to play. It had been so long since she'd played. They ate in silence.

"You told me you like to be flogged," he commented, sitting back in the chair and watching her with those intense blue eyes.

"I do." She pushed away her empty plate and took a sip of water.

"Tell me more, Sara. Do you like it soft? Hard? What is your pleasure?"

A shiver chased up her spine at his words. "Since we've never played before, I'd say let's start off soft and go from there."

He nodded and looked pleased. "I can do that." He stood. "I shall return in a moment."

Sara admired his fine ass in the tight black pants as he walked out of the room. She shifted in her chair. Anticipation danced along her skin. Standing up, she walked over to the table he'd set in the middle of the room.

It was adjustable; she ran her fingers over the leather. It was soft and supple. She noted the restraints hanging off the sides as another shiver flowed through her body. They were really going to do this. She heard footsteps and turned to see Hassan returning to the room.

Her gaze zeroed in on his hands. He was carrying several different types of floggers. Her nipples tightened and her core clenched.

Hassan strode over to another small table she hadn't noticed. It was covered with a white cloth. He laid the floggers out on the table. "Come here."

The command in his voice made her knees weak. She stepped over to him and glanced down at the floggers. "Rabbit." She forced herself not to reach out and touch it. She raised her head and looked at him for permission.

Desire darkened his eyes. "You may touch them."

Her fingers touched the soft tails of the rabbit flogger, then the elk flogger. That would be heavier, but not too heavy. Next came a suede flogger, it would sting when it hit her skin. She'd felt one before.

The next flogger sent a tremor up her spine. Not exactly fear, but not exactly excitement either. A braided flogger. She'd only had one like this used on her once. The darn thing was heavy. It had a thuddy feeling, but one heck of a sting. Her body flushed with the thought of feeling it against her bare ass. Next was a bull flogger. She'd seen one before, but never played with one.

She stared at the last flogger on the table. She'd never seen anything like it. Each tail was braided, then they were put together in one flogger. She wasn't even sure what it was made of. "I've never seen one like this," she said, pointing to it.

"That is a braided bull flogger." Hassan reached around her and lifted the flogger. "Each tail is individually braided and wrapped, then joined to make one flogger. Thuddy and stingy at the same time."

He ran the tails over her arm, and her stomach tingled with nerves. It was heavy, and her ass tightened at the thought of being flogged with something so heavy and yet so wicked.

"For tonight, we'll start with the rabbit, move to the elk, and, if needed, to the suede. I wanted you to see what I had available."

Sara nodded, her body already anticipating the feel of the floggers against her skin. The soft touch of the rabbit, to the more thuddy feel of elk, to the slight sting of the suede.

"Safe words?"

"Camel, slow down. Fox, stop."

He nodded. "Take off your robe." His deep, husky order had her sucking in a shaky breath, but she complied. Undoing the tie, she allowed the robe to fall open, then she slipped it off. Hassan took it from her nerveless fingers and laid it over a chair. His gaze raked over her body.

Sara fought against squirming. "So beautiful." His voice was low and husky. "Now over to the table. On your stomach."

She padded over to the table, wondering how this was going to work. But she followed his orders. She climbed up onto the table and lay down. She turned her head so she could see Hassan.

He moved over to the table. "Arms over head." His warm

fingers closed over her wrists the second she followed his orders. His hand dipped, then the cool leather restraints were placed over her wrists. "Okay?" he asked. He ran his finger underneath the restraint, checking the tightness.

"Yes ... Sir." They hadn't really discussed what she should call him.

"I like that." He ran his hand down her spine before cupping her ass and squeezing. Then his touch moved over the back of her thighs and to her ankles.

He restrained her ankles, then, to her surprise, pulled another pair of restraints right above her knees. "Don't panic," he said. Before she could ask him what he meant, the table moved beneath her lower body.

Sara let out a small cry, but Hassan was there, his hand on her lower back, softly stroking her skin. A rolled-up soft towel was slipped between her belly and the table. It caused her ass to raise even more, and her legs were angled down.

"I've adjusted the table to raise your ass, but to put your legs down out of my way. Think of this as a special spanking bench."

She bit her tongue not to let go with what she really thought. She wouldn't have thought Hassan could be so devious. She'd underestimated him, and she wouldn't do that again.

"Are you comfortable? Anything hurt?"

"No, Sir." She shifted her hips as his palm caressed her ass again, then ... slap.

Her ass tightened and then relaxed before his next slap. Her breathing increased as he paddled one cheek and then the other. Her skin heated. When he stopped his cool palms caressed her hot butt.

"Smooth skin, turned pink by my touch. Let's see what the flogger can do."

Sara fought her own inclination to tense up. She barely heard the whoosh before the rabbit flogger touched her ass. The soft caress of the rabbit fur made her sigh.

Its slight stinging feel against her skin allowed her to slowly let her muscles relax and let go of the tension she'd been holding inside since yesterday. She groaned when Hassan caressed her ass cheeks, soothing them.

"Like that, do you?" His voice was deeper than before.

"Yes, Sir." She let out a sigh as his touch disappeared, but excitement flowed through her veins. She couldn't see him. Was he getting the next flogger? The elk one?

"Are you anticipating what I'm doing?"

"Yes, Sir." She was, and she wouldn't lie to him. If this was going to work they needed to be honest with each other.

He chuckled. "For tonight, I'll stick with what we talked about. In the future, I'll mix it up. I don't want you becoming too compliant."

"No chance of that, Sir." The elk flogger struck. The thuddy feeling had her biting her lower lip before the sting vibrated through her body. Her back arched, and she lifted her ass higher.

"You are so responsive." Hassan's voice was soft and husky.

Each swing of the flogger against her skin sent her deeper and deeper into a relaxed state. All her worries about the clinics, and the stress about the reporters and being connected to the royal family, all floated away. The pattern of flogging, then Hassan's soothing touch, and then more flogging, didn't change. She drifted away in a floating sea of sensation.

"Sara?" Hassan rubbed her back and shoulders, then he undid the wrist restraints. He'd stopped flogging her within a minute of her hitting subspace, and then he undid her leg restraints. Lord, this woman was beautiful and responsive.

"More, Sir." Her voice was soft and her eyes closed.

"Not tonight." He grabbed the blanket he'd set out earlier, then slipped the towel from underneath her stomach. He shook the blanket out and laid it over her body, then carefully he lifted her into his arms.

He sat down on the sofa with Sara in his lap, tucking the blanket around her so she wouldn't get cold. He cradled her against his chest. "You are so beautiful, so responsive. Perfect." He kept murmuring the words, reassuring her.

He'd learned to flog when he was in England, but never had a sub react like Sara. She'd gone into subspace rather quickly, but when he glanced at the clock he realized they'd been playing longer than he'd thought.

He got a high from watching the way she reacted to his

actions, and some might call that Dom space. He was always aware of her breathing, the color of her skin, and where the flogger struck. Plus he never put too much power behind it.

He turned his gaze to her face. Her eyes were still closed, but her chest rose and fell, deep and steady. Good. He rested his head against the back of the sofa and closed his eyes. Their next session he'd see how she liked his toys.

A short time later, Sara squirmed in his arms, and Hassan opened his eyes. He must have dozed off. He shook his head. This woman allowed him to relax like no other had. He turned his head to see her watching him. "Hello, sweetheart." He brushed his lips over hers.

"Ummm, hi." Her voice was quiet. "Sorry about that."

"About what? Going into subspace?" She nodded, and his lips tilted up. "Never be sorry. It's an honor you trusted me so much to let go. I certainly didn't expect it on our first time."

Her eyes brightened. "I didn't, either. You didn't mind?"

"Why would I mind?" He frowned. Something was off here. "It's one of the greatest gifts a sub can give her Dom. Did someone tell you otherwise?"

Sara shook her head. "Not really told, but I felt the weight of my old Dom's disappointment when I would hit subspace."

"He was an idiot." He brushed his lips over hers once again. "How are you feeling?" He didn't think he'd been too rough with her.

"Wonderful." She gave him a shy smile.

"Have you always gone into subspace from flogging?" He wanted to know more about her play before him.

"Not in the beginning, at least."

"Why flogging? Why not just play?" He was curious. She wasn't a masochist, or she wouldn't have gone into subspace so easily. And he was no sadist, although some of his patients might say otherwise.

"I'm not sure. I discovered by accident it was soothing for me. I feel the sting and the thud of the flogger, but most of the time it's minute—the pain, I mean. The flogger allows me to let go of all my stress and my worries. I'm surprised how fast I went into subspace. It usually takes a lot longer."

"How long does it usually take you?"

"Usually the suede flogger, before I fully let go."

Hassan nodded, but he suspected there was something else affecting her. He wasn't going to worry about that now. Instead, he stood with her in his arms and carried her into his bedroom.

"Hassan?" He laid her on the bed.

"Shhh." He pressed his fingers over her lips. When she nodded, he went back out to the sitting room and blew out the candles before returning to the bedroom. He walked over to Sara, picked her up, and carried her into the bathroom. "Shower to get the sweat off and then we'll rest."

She nodded. He turned on the shower and stripped off his pants. His cock was jutting up. Her eyes widened.

"Ummmm, you're quite large."

"As if you didn't know that already."

Her cheeks turned pink and he grinned.

"In," he said, gesturing toward the open shower doors.

Sara let the blanket drop and stepped into the now-steaming enclosure. The hot water hit her skin and made her shiver. Hassan climbed in behind her.

"Too hot." He reached around her and twisted the knobs. "Better?"

"Yes." Her brain froze when he put his arms around her waist. They'd kissed, he'd seen her naked, she'd stroked his cock, so why was this so different? She wasn't sure, but feeling his hard cock against her skin made it seem more real.

"What is it?" Those strong hands cupped her hips, turning her to face him. The water caressed her spine.

"I ... " What could she say? She shrugged her shoulders.

"Sara." He cupped her chin when she lowered her eyes. "Look at me."

She forced herself to look at him. There was tenderness and concern in his eyes. Her heart pounded.

"Better," he said. "Now, tell me what is bothering you?"

"I'm not sure." She frowned. "I mean, this seems so intimate."

Hassan laughed, and her frown deepened. So like a man not to understand.

"Sweetheart." He ran his fingers over her cheek before cupping the nape of her neck. "I love how comfortable you are in your own skin. You weren't afraid to be naked with me or to play with me. You are a treasure. A sexy, beautiful treasure."

Her eyes misted. His voice was full of sincerity and pride. No man had ever talked to her like this. Not even her play Dom.

"Now, let's shower and catch a nap. I have a feeling there will be a family dinner tonight."

"But aren't your parents away?"

"Won't stop Malik from calling us all together." He kissed her nose. "Now tilt your head back so your hair gets wet. I'm going to wash your hair."

Sara woke the next morning and stretched. Muscles protested at the movement, and a smile curved her lips as the events of her time with Hassan yesterday filtered in. She opened her eyes and blinked. This wasn't her room. Then she remembered that after their shower together, they'd napped in Hassan's bed.

When they'd woken late in the afternoon, they'd both dressed for the dinner Malik had called, but after dinner, Hassan had led her back to his room. He undressed her with soft touches and pulled her into bed.

He'd stroked her back until she fell asleep. She slid her legs over the side of the mattress and sat up. A white robe lay on the chair, and she smiled. Hassan was so thoughtful, but it was more than that. Sara stood, slipped the robe on, and walked to the bathroom.

After splashing water on her face, brushing her teeth—Hassan had left a new toothbrush on the counter for her—and running his comb through her hair, she went to see where Hassan was.

She stood in the doorway to the sitting room. He'd put the room back together. No traces of the table or his floggers remained. Hassan sat on the sofa with two pots on the coffee table, and he was reading what looked like a medical journal.

"Good morning," she said softly so as not to startle him.

"Good morning." He set the journal aside, stood, and smiled. "How are you feeling this morning?"

"Deliciously rested."

Hassan laughed and patted the seat next to him. "Come sit down and have some tea. Then we can discuss our day."

"Our day?" She sat down and accepted the cup of tea he poured for her. She took a sip and then looked at him. "How did you know how I took my tea?" It had just the right amount of sweetness to it.

"Three teaspoons of sugar, not super healthy for you, but I understand. As for our day, Malik, Khalid, and I had another talk this morning."

Sara sighed. Why did she have a feeling this wasn't good?

"Khalid is bringing in more guards so we'll be protected when we go out to the villages to work on the clinics."

"Oh, that was it." She took another sip of her tea before setting her cup down. Then she caught sight of the time. "Oh, crap."

"What?"

"I forgot I need to go with Catherine to the dressmakers today. I've got to go get ready." She stood up. "There goes your plan for today."

"My plans can wait." Hassan nodded. "I haven't heard anyone knock on your door."

"That's because I've still got fifteen minutes." She brushed her hair back from her face.

"Until tonight, then." Hassan drew her into his arms and kissed her.

Coffee and the tangy taste of citrus filled her as their tongues mingled and danced. She melted into his embrace. This was where she wanted to be, in his arms, his bed, his life. The thoughts filtered through her brain, but they didn't scare her.

When he broke the kiss she was clinging to him. "I don't want to leave."

"You can't disappoint Catherine. Plus I need to run to the hospital and check on things."

"All right." Together they walked to his door.

"Shall I escort you to your room?" he asked.

"It's just next door. Besides, I think it's enough of a scandal if anyone sees me, in a robe, going from your room to mine."

He laughed. "Nothing is totally secret in the palace."

"What?" She gripped his arm, hard. "Are you telling me the guards and your family know about our play?"

"No. They know we're a couple and you spent the night in my room."

Her fingers relaxed. That she could handle. She wanted to keep their play private. "Thank goodness."

Hassan framed her face with his palms. "Our play is between us and only us, unless we make the decision to tell anyone. Everything else, well, sorry, that's kind of an open secret."

"I can live with that. I need to go."

"Yes." He took her lips again in a hard brief kiss, then opened the door. "Go before I change my mind and keep you here."

"Tease." She nipped at his lips before slipping out of his embrace and making her way to her room. Hassan watched her. She opened her door and waved to him before stepping inside.

Sara hurried into her bedroom, tossing off the robe and getting dressed. She had just finished her hair when someone knocked on her door. She opened it to see Najah waiting. "Good morning, Lady Sara. Crown Princess Catherine is waiting for you."

"Thank you, Najah." Sara found her purse and followed Najah to the car. He held the door open for her, and she climbed inside to see Catherine smile.

"Good morning," Catherine said.

"Morning." The doors closed.

"So, tell me about last night with Hassan," Catherine said as they drove toward the marketplace.

"Is there nothing sacred?" Sara grinned.

"No. Spill, girlfriend. I want all the details."

"I don't remember you giving me any details." Sara crossed her arms over her chest, trying not to laugh.

Catherine's cheeks turned red and she gave Sara a shy smile. "You got me." They both laughed.

"We had a good play session, showered, napped, had dinner last night, and then went to bed."

"Together?"

"Yes, but we slept. No sex."

Catherine frowned.

"It will come, it was our first time together." Sara wasn't lying, because in a way it was, but they'd already been intimate on so many levels.

"I'm sure you'll have lots of time together." The car stopped and they climbed out.

Sara looked around. They were on the edge of the marketplace. The colorful awnings and tents made her smile. While she hadn't had a lot of time to explore, she'd walked around the area and loved the sights and smells.

Samir and Najah walked up to them. They both bowed. Catherine and Sara giggled. "Please, guys, informal time," Catherine said.

"This is going to be an interesting fitting with body-guards," Sara said, walking with Catherine.

"They'll stay outside," Catherine said, looking over her shoulder at Samir.

"Of course we will, Crown Princess."

Catherine frowned, then sighed. "I need to train them better."

Another giggle left Sara's lips. It was so good to be around her best friend. She was more carefree and relaxed. Of course, a lot of that could have come from playing with Hassan.

"This is it," Catherine said, pulling her to a stop in front of a small shop. Bolts of fabric were in the window. "Stay out here." Catherine pulled her through the entrance.

"Crown Princess, Lady Sara," a small woman said when they entered. "I'm so happy you were able to come today." She waved her wrinkled hands toward the back of the store. "Please, this way, I have refreshments and then, Crown Princess, you can try on your dress for the fitting."

"Thank you, Ramala," Catherine said, as together they followed the shopkeeper to the back.

Sara and Catherine sat down on the overstuffed sofa as a young girl came in with a tray and set it down. A silver teapot, two cups, milk and sugar. Then another girl came in and set down a tray filled with fruit, cheese, and nuts.

"Thank you," Sara said. The girls scurried off.

"Crown Princess, if you're ready," Ramala said.

"Be right back." Catherine stood and went behind a set of curtains.

Sara poured the tea and popped a piece of cheddar cheese into her mouth. She hadn't had breakfast this morning and had barely gotten a cup of tea down before she'd realized she had to leave.

Fifteen minutes later, Sara had drunk two cups of tea and eaten half of the fruit and cheese. The curtains parted, and Catherine stepped out.

Sara jumped to her feet. "Oh, my God, Catherine, that's absolutely beautiful." When Catherine had first told her about the concept of the dress, Sara had thought it sounded good, but wondered how it would look. Now she knew.

The white fabric flowed over Catherine's curves, highlighting them, but it was more than that. Sara didn't know what kind of fabric had been used, but the light glittered off the dress.

"Ramala did a fantastic job," Catherine said.

"It was my honor, Crown Princess. Now, if you hold still for a few minutes, let me pin a few places, and then we can put it back on the model and I can show you how I'm going to incorporate the royal colors."

Thirty minutes later, Catherine was back in her normal clothes and sitting next to Sara on the sofa. "Someone was hungry," Catherine said, gesturing toward the half-empty tray.

Sara's face grew warm. "I missed breakfast."

"I bet." Catherine poured them both more tea as Ramala brought out the dress on a mannequin, along with several lengths of different fabrics.

Within minutes, Sara was stunned. Ramala had taken the fabrics and draped them around the dress. The royal colors enhanced rather than detracted from the beauty of the dress.

"Now, the bodice will be made of lace, as well as your train. There will be pearl buttons down the back, and the fabric I used is light, so you shouldn't have any issues getting too warm or too cold," Ramala said.

"It's absolutely beautiful," Sara said. "You are going to make the most beautiful bride, Catherine."

"And Malik a handsome groom." Catherine grinned. "Ramala, do you have a Sara's dress as well?"

"Of course. Lady Sara, if you would come with me, please."

Sara stood and followed the shopkeeper behind the curtains. The room was filled with fabrics and mannequins.

"Lady Sara, if you would please undress, I will get the dress for the wedding." The shopkeeper walked behind another set of curtains.

Sara toed off her shoes, then took off her jeans and blouse. Ramala arrived back with a deep red dress. She held the dress up. The back wasn't finished yet, so all Sara had to do was lift her arms and Ramala slid the fabric on.

The cloth caressed her skin as it went on. Soft and silky,

almost like silk. Ramala moved behind Sara, gathering up the fabric.

"Good, we have plenty of cloth to work with if we need to. I'm going to pin the back so you can walk out and show the Crown Princess."

"That's fine." Sara stood still until Ramala was done. Then together they walked out. Catherine set her teacup down and stared at Sara.

"Is it that bad?"

"It's perfect. That color is just perfect on you," Catherine said, clapping her hands.

"Are you positive?" Sara wasn't sure about the deep red.

"Let me drape the royal colors over you, and then I'll bring the mirror so you can look," Ramala said.

Sara waited anxiously as Ramala wrapped more fabric over her, then she yelled for the young girl to bring out the full-length mirror. The girl came out with the mirror and stepped in front of Sara, and Sara's jaw dropped open.

The dress was more a deep maroon than she'd thought, and with the royal colors draped around her, they brought out the color of her eyes, and her hair looked lighter too. "Oh, my goodness." Sara's hand fluttered to her chest. "This is absolutely gorgeous. Ramala, you are a true artist with fabric."

"Thank you, Lady Sara. Hold still for a moment, and I'll pin the hem and a few other places."

Sara nodded, and Ramala did her magic before Sara

went back to change. She and Catherine both thanked Ramala for the refreshments and complimented her on her work before leaving. Sara and Catherine left the shop with Samir and Najah behind them.

"I'm glad we got to go do this," Catherine said as they walked.

"Me too."

Catherine stopped at a shop. "I need to go in here."

Samir let out a groan, and Sara looked at him before following Catherine into the shop. Sara burst out laughing. No wonder Samir had groaned. It was a bookstore. Catherine could easily spend hours in one; then again, so could she.

Four hours later, they returned to the palace. Samir and Najah insisted on carrying their purchases. Sara had been good; she'd only picked up three books, and two of them were on Bashir's history. Catherine, on the other hand ... Sara shook her head. Her friend had picked up at least twenty books, including some the shopkeeper had special-ordered for her.

They were laughing as they walked into the palace, but their laughter died when they found Hassan and Malik waiting for them.

"Hi, honey." Catherine walked up to Malik and gave him a kiss, then pulled back. "What's going on?"

Hassan stepped forward and took Sara's hands in his. A sense of dread filled her. Hassan's blue eyes were dim with worry.

"Seems no matter what we do, the press is always two steps ahead of us." Malik put his arm around Catherine.

"What have they done now?" The disgust in Catherine's voice made Sara wince, but Sara understood it.

"Let's go sit down," Hassan said, guiding Sara to the main sitting room. Sara was surprised to see Khalid and Rafi standing off to the side.

"This has something to do with us, doesn't it?" Sara whispered. Had someone found out about their playing together?

"In a way, yes." Hassan tugged her down onto the sofa with him. "I do not want you to take responsibility."

"For what?" Sara's stomach cramped.

Hassan glanced up, and Khalid stepped forward. He held a newspaper out and handed it to Hassan. Sara braced herself, and Hassan opened it.

While the picture was grainy, it was obvious someone had taken it from inside the dressmaker's store today. It showed Sara in nothing but her underwear. Her blood froze. She glanced up at Hassan, then her gaze went to everyone else. "How?"

"How what?" Catherine asked, anger in her voice.

Hassan handed the paper to Malik before putting his arm around Sara's shoulders. "This isn't your fault."

"Those sons of a donkey."

Sara burst out laughing at Catherine's words. "I think they're worse than that. And please don't insult the donkeys."

She leaned into Hassan's embrace, glad to have him on her side. "What are we going to do?"

"Get to the bottom of this," Hassan replied.

"Who else was at the dressmaker's shop?" Malik asked.

"Samir and Najah waited outside. Just Ramala and her two assistants," Catherine said.

"I'm on it." Khalid left the room and Rafi followed.

"Where are they going?" Sara's stomach tumbled over and over.

"To see Ramala," Malik said.

"Ramala wouldn't have done something like this," Catherine protested.

"I agree. She's been making garments for the royal family for years. It had to be one of her assistants."

"But why?" Sara asked. Why would someone want to do this to her? Let alone Hassan and the royal family.

"To embarrass the family, maybe." Hassan squeezed her shoulders.

"I don't get it." Sara shook her head. "I'm just a family friend. Why go to all this trouble?"

"You are so much more than a family friend." He leaned down and brushed a kiss across her lips. "And don't you forget it."

Her cheeks heated. Thankfully, only Catherine and Malik were in the room.

"Khalid and Rafi will get to the bottom of this. Now all we can do is wait," Malik said, then he looked at his future wife.

"I have some work to do in my office. Will you come with me?"

"Of course." The two left the room.

Sara looked at Hassan. "What are we going to do?"

"Wait. I have confidence in my brothers. But while we do that," he said, then brushed another kiss across her lips, "why don't we go to my room?"

"And what do you have in mind?" Sara's blood heated at the desire flaring in Hassan's eyes.

"Just a little play time."

"I think I can handle that."

Several hours later, Hassan wore a satisfied smile as he and Sara entered the sitting room once again. Sara was so responsive to him.

"Well?" he asked, seeing Khalid standing with Malik and Catherine.

"It was one of the assistants," Khalid said.

"Did she say why?" Sara asked.

"Yes." Malik bit out, and it was then Hassan noticed his brother's clenched fists. "The assistant had only been hired a few days ago."

Hassan tried to be patient, but he looked at Khalid. "The girl told me Kalif asked her to take the pictures," Khalid said.

"What the hell?" Hassan drew his hand through his hair.

Why was Kalif so damn interested in Sara?

"Wait, I'm confused," Sara said.

"Please sit." Khalid gestured for them to be seated. Sara sat in the chair Hassan directed her to, but he stood behind her and placed his hands on her shoulders. If he sat he might explode.

Catherine and Malik sat on the sofa together, Catherine caressing the back of Malik's clenched fist until he relaxed and their fingers entwined.

Khalid knelt down in front of Sara. "For some reason, Kalif sees you as a threat. From what Rafi and I got out of the girl, Kalif paid her to get pictures of you. He was hoping for nude pictures. No matter how much we search for Kalif, he seems to have disappeared."

Shock rocked through Sara's body. Hassan tightened his fingers on her shoulders. "For a fitting?"

"That wouldn't have happened," Catherine said. "Ramala is careful. If she needed you totally undressed she would have taken you to a private room rather than the dressing room."

"I agree. Ramala was extremely upset about what happened." Khalid took Sara's hand. "Little sister, do not let this bother you. I will find out what Kalif is up to."

"Khalid, did the young woman say why she took the pictures for Kalif?" Sara asked. Hassan had wondered the same thing.

"Yes." Khalid sighed, released Sara's hand, and stood. "I

know you're working as fast as you can, but we need to do something about the outlying villages. The girl explained her father was addicted to opium, and Kalif told her if she didn't do this for him, he'd make sure her father suffered."

Hassan swore. This was something he'd been worried about. The stronger Kalif and his band got, the worse it was going to get for the villages.

"I can't force the villagers to take our help. They are a proud people." Malik let out a heavy breath.

"Proud or not, we need to do more outreach," Hassan said. He stepped away from Sara and began pacing.

"What if Hassan and I go visit one of the villages?" Sara said softly.

He stopped pacing and stared at her. "Visit?"

"Yes, we could take a mobile clinic."

"That's not a bad idea," Khalid said.

"What are you thinking?" Hassan asked.

"We take another doctor and nurse with us and go to one of the villages close to Kalif's territory. We show the people we're here for them, to help them with whatever issues they are having. Hassan," she said, and looked up at him before continuing, "you are part of the royal family. I'm sure that will please a lot of the villagers."

Malik nodded. "It could work."

"Yes," Khalid agreed. "We'll need extra security and this will not be announced. You will just show up; this way, Kalif can't plan anything."

Hassan rubbed his forehead. "Agreed. A surprise visit, then we can get a good idea of what is actually happening in the villages." He glanced at Sara. "I'm not sure how safe this trip will be." Maybe he could convince her to stay at the palace.

"It was my idea, so you're not leaving me here." She took his hand in hers. "It will be fine, Hassan. There will be security."

Hassan liked the idea, but he didn't like the idea of putting Sara in danger. He nodded. They would discuss this tonight.

Hassan slid the old key into the lock. After a session with his brothers, they had a plan in place. Now he wanted to talk to Sara, but she'd locked her door again. He searched out Khalid, and his brother had found one of the old keys for Hassan just in case Sara had locked her door. She had.

He still hadn't gotten to the bottom of why Sara had locked the door. The lock clicked, and he slipped inside her room. After closing the door behind him, he dropped the key into his pocket.

The sitting area was semi-dark, although a small lamp on the table was on. "Sara," he said, but there was no reply. She'd said she'd wait up for him, but the planning session had gone on longer than he'd wanted.

He crossed the room and stopped at her bedroom door. A vision greeted him. Sara was in bed, her blonde hair spread out over her pillow. She wore a skimpy nightgown and was sound asleep.

This didn't surprise him. She must be tired after everything that had gone on today. He was glad now he'd stopped in his room to change clothes. Within a few steps he was at the side of her bed.

Quietly, he slipped off his shoes and robe, laying the robe on the chair before he pulled back the covers.

"Cold," Sara mumbled, tugging at the covers.

Hassan slipped beneath the covers and reached for her, but she was already turning toward him. A smile creased his face when she snuggled up against him.

"Nice. Warm," she mumbled.

He frowned. She was shivering. The room wasn't that cold. He slipped his arms around her and held her against his body. He pulled the covers over her. Tonight he was content to hold her.

Hassan stared at the ceiling, replaying the conversations with his brothers from earlier. Kalif was becoming a bigger issue than they'd realized. Malik had been trying to get a handle on the problem quietly, but now, with the break-in at the palace and the pictures of Sara, quietly wasn't working so well.

Kalif hadn't wanted Malik to become king, but there wasn't a way he could stop it. So now he just pumped more and more opium out. The younger generation was lured into working for Kalif by money. But there were better ways for them.

The country had its exports, and if need be, they'd make sure the villages had what they needed to start whatever they wanted to grow or raise to export. It would help the villagers feel productive and be part of the process.

A medical clinic would help. He could hire doctors and nurses to staff them, and once the addiction center opened, the harder cases could be referred there. He wanted to do so much more for his people, but they had to accept his help. As the minister of health, he took his job seriously.

Sara shifted and brought his attention back to her. Could he convince her to stay here and not go with him to the village? Khalid had assured him the danger would be minimal, but he was still worried.

"How did you get in here?" Her sleepy voice made him smile. Her green eyes were staring up at him languidly.

"Key." He kissed her forehead.

"Sneaky."

He smiled. "Go back to sleep. We both have a busy day tomorrow."

"Okay." She snuggled against his body and in a few seconds she was sound asleep.

He grinned. Tomorrow was going to be a busy day of planning and getting supplies for the trip. He should heed his own advice and sleep. He wanted to make love to Sara, but they both needed to rest. It was going to be a busy couple of days. Closing his eyes, he relaxed, enjoying having Sara in his arms and his life.

Sara woke feeling toasty warm. This was nice. So often, even in a bed with lots of covers, she was cold. An old feeling from her past that never seemed to go away. But it was nice to wake up feeling warm and settled.

She shifted. Her lashes rose. There was a reason she was so toasty; she was being held against a masculine chest. She tilted her head. So she hadn't dreamed he'd gotten into her room and bed. He'd mentioned a key. Sneaky guy.

Carefully, she maneuvered her body until she could see the clock. It was only six. But she was wide awake. She slipped out of his embrace and out of bed. She'd get a shower and be ready when Hassan awoke.

He wanted her to stay at the palace while he went out to the villages, but that wasn't going to happen. It was her idea. Plus she suspected some of the women might be more comfortable talking with a woman, especially one not of their own country. Grabbing clean underclothes, Sara stepped into the bathroom and showered quickly.

Hot steam filled the room by the time she was done. She grabbed a towel off the heated rack. She was going to miss this when she went back home. Her body froze in place.

While she and Hassan hadn't really discussed much beyond exploring their attraction to each other, she wasn't sure she wanted to leave Bashir. She really enjoyed being around her best friend, but also volunteering at the hospital. Plus there would be more outreach clinics to set up. She wasn't going to dwell on this right now. She had more important things to think about.

Sara dressed and then strolled out to the bedroom. Hassan was sitting up in bed. "Good morning," she said.

"You took a shower without me."

Hot tendrils of desire shot through her body at his husky words. "I thought you'd appreciate a little extra sleep."

"I did." He stood and stretched. Sara admired the way his muscles contracted and then released. Damn, this man was hot. "Let me go grab a quick shower and dress. Then we'll go down to breakfast."

"Sure." She walked over to the small vanity and sat down. She pulled the towel off her hair and picked up her brush. Hassan came up behind her. "I thought you were going to take a shower?"

"I was, but I don't want to leave you, and I don't have any clothes here." He took the brush from her hand and began running it through her wet hair. He stopped to gently remove any tangles before brushing again.

Sara closed her eyes. It was soothing to have him brush her hair. Soothing and erotic. Her nipples tightened, and her tongue darted out to wet her lips.

Hassan let out a groan, and she opened her eyes. His gaze was on her mouth. "I'd better go before I throw you onto the bed and take you the way I want to."

"What's stopping you?"

He set her brush on the table, his blue eyes blazing. "Time," he murmured, before taking her lips in a hard, fast kiss. Before she knew it, he had broken the kiss and left the room.

Her fingers flittered to her lips, and then the door shut. Her mouth throbbed, and her pussy clenched with unfilled desire. Tonight.

Sara let out a sigh when she stepped out of the shower that night. She'd taken the shower to wash off her tiredness. The day had gone quickly. They'd gathered supplies and personnel for their trip to the village. Hassan had tried several times to talk her out of going, and she'd refused.

Because there were things about her past he didn't know about, visiting the villages was important to her. She wanted to see for herself how bad the opium crisis was. Slipping on her robe, she walked into her bedroom. She should be tired, but she wasn't. Maybe a cup of tea would settle her down.

After filling the electric teakettle with water and plugging it in, she contemplated her life. Hassan was nothing like her ex, Peter. Hassan was sweet, generous, and in tune with her and her body. He was able to send her into full-fledged desire with one smolder, look from those beautiful blue eyes of his.

He was also aware of how hard he could push her during play. Taking their relationship to the next level was a natural progression. She glanced at the small calendar hanging on the wall. How long had she been here? Just a few weeks, but it seemed much longer.

She'd hoped tonight they could be together, but Hassan had told her not to wait up for him. He was going over security details with his brothers. The kettle whistled, and Sara turned it off. She made herself a cup of tea, then wandered to the overstuffed chair and made herself comfortable.

She hadn't told Hassan her reasons for wanting to go to the village with him. It was more than setting up the clinic. She knew what it was like to be addicted to opioids. Those nice painkillers made from opium—she'd been addicted to them during her first year at university.

So she understood what some of the people were going through, and she could also help them understand why treatment was a good idea. If it hadn't been for her mentor, she probably never would have kicked the drugs.

Now the medical field was learning more, and doctors were much more careful about giving out painkillers. After kicking her addiction, Sara had done everything she could to educate herself, and she understood why a country like Bashir might have an issue.

Poppy growing was easy, and the money was good. And

from what she'd gleaned from conversations with Hassan and his brothers, the older tribes didn't want to let go of the old ways.

The royal family worked hard to help the people of Bashir and make the country prosper. Was it more about money? Or was there more about politics?

A knock on the balcony window made her jump. With caution, Sara walked to the doors and pulled back the curtain to see out. Hassan stood there.

Sara unlocked the door and opened it. "What are you doing out here?"

"I saw your light on. Is everything okay?"

"Yes. I wasn't ready to go to sleep yet." She shook her head and stepped back. "You might as well come in before someone sees you and sends the household into a panic."

Hassan slipped inside, then closed the door and locked it. In a way she was glad he was here, and in another she wasn't sure at all.

"Would you like a cup of tea? Or I can make you coffee?"

He framed her face with his palms, his warm touch caressing her skin and sending shivers of desire and anticipation through her body.

"What is keeping you up?" There was genuine concern in his eyes.

"Lots of things." Time to clear the air, so to speak.

"Is it because I want you to stay here and not come with me to the village?" He released her.

"That's part of it. There is a reason I need to go with you. Things in my past that I don't like to talk about."

"What if I tell you your past doesn't matter?"

Sara tilted her head. "Our past makes us what we are today."

"I agree with you on that, but my past hasn't been stellar either."

Sara let out a laugh. "Really, Hassan? I know you're the third son, but you grew up, as far as I can tell, in a loved and secure environment."

Hassan's lips turned up. "If we're going to have this kind of talk, let's get comfortable."

She nodded and started for the sofa. Hassan caught her hand and guided her to the bedroom. He dimmed the lights, then led her to the bed. They'd slept in each other arms, so there was nothing wrong with him in her bed.

She climbed into bed, Hassan shed his robe and followed her. Once he settled in, he pulled her into his arms, her head resting on his shoulder.

"You're right. I grew up loved and secure. Didn't you?"

They hadn't talked much about their past. "Partially." Sara struggled with the words. "My parents are older. I was a late-in-life baby."

"No brothers or sisters?"

"No. Not that I didn't want them, but basically my parents never expected to have children. I was a surprise to them." She scrunched up her nose. "My mom was a housewife and my dad worked at the local factory."

"Did you grow up in London?"

"No, outside of it. We lived in a pretty small town, and to be honest, I couldn't wait to leave." She'd always dreamed of living in London, and she'd worked hard every day to make her dreams come true.

"I can understand that." He shifted. "Did you always want to be a nurse?"

"Not really, but when I was in school my teachers realized I had an affinity for not only helping others, but math and chemistry."

"Those could assist you in many careers."

"True, but I loved helping people feel better and watching them gain confidence." She thought back to her time in school and smiled. She had good memories of her friends and teachers.

"Why do I have a feeling you aced everything you tried, including your A levels?"

"I did." A shiver of ice raced up her spine. "After my A levels I was in an accident."

Hassan stiffened, and his arms tightened around her. "What kind of accident?"

"Car." She took an unsteady breath. "I'd been out celebrating with friends, and another friend offered me a ride home. I didn't know he was impaired. He crashed the car."

"What happened?" His voice was soft and helped give her

the courage to continue.

"I was lucky. I broke my leg and had a concussion. My friend the driver survived with minor cuts and bruises." She inhaled. "His older brother was in the passenger seat. He hadn't put his seatbelt on. He was ejected from the car and died instantly."

"I'm so sorry," he said, his voice quiet.

"The inquiry was horrendous. I wouldn't have gotten into the car had I known he had drunk too much." She hadn't talked about this in a long time. "When he was brought up to the magistrates who heard his case, he was lucky. I testified for him. He was a good friend, and I thought he'd suffered enough knowing his brother died."

"You are a good friend." He brushed his palm over the back of her head. "When I was fourteen, Rafi and I decided it would be fun to ride out into the desert and live like our ancestors."

Sara gave a little laugh. "I bet that went over well with your parents."

"Oh, yeah." He chuckled. "They let Rafi and me stay out in the desert for several days. It wasn't like we were alone. Our bodyguards were with us."

"They didn't make you come back home?"

"No, their orders were to protect us, not make us mind. Rafi and I had no clue what we were doing." He turned his head, and his breath ruffled her hair. "After four days, two of those not eating, we decided to come home."

"What did your parents do?"

"Mom hugged us and made sure we got fed. Dad, well, let's say we got lectured and hugged."

"Your parents are so down to earth. I mean, for being a king and queen."

"Mom came from London. She met Dad when she was working for the UK ambassador as a secretary."

"A romantic fairytale come to life." Her life was anything but a fairytale, but lying here in bed, she could almost believe in one.

"In some ways. Finish your story, please. You aced your A levels."

"My leg healed, and I started at the university to get my nursing degree. I met Peter, who was a year away from starting his residency as a doctor."

"A match made in heaven," Hassan said dryly.

"You would think so, but fate has a way of making her will known."

"What do you mean?"

She closed her eyes, then opened them. "At the end of my first year at the university, I realized I had a problem. A very big problem." She tilted her head back and concentrated on his handsome face. "When I broke my leg they put me on painkillers."

"You were in a lot of pain."

"Yes, then there was rehab, and I was studying so I wouldn't fall behind when I started at the university." Her stomach churned. "At the time none of us knew better. Pain was my constant companion, so the doctors kept giving me painkillers, or, should I say, opioids."

Hassan sucked in a breath, and she plunged on. "I'm not proud of it, but I became addicted to them. At the end of my first year at the university, I realized how much they were affecting my life. I broke things off with Peter so he could continue on with his studies and went to my mentor for help."

"And he helped you?" His fingers caressed the nape of her neck. Sara took comfort in his touch.

"Yes." So far Hassan seemed to understand, but he was a doctor. What did the man think?

"I told him what was going on. The first thing he did was take all my prescription drugs away from me, then he found me a rehabilitation unit I could go to, and he talked to the university so I could take some time off without being penalized."

"The rehab helped?"

"It did, along with my mentor's support. Once I was clean, I went back to the university with a new understanding. I began to study addiction because I didn't want to fall into the trap ever again. That was when I discovered kink."

She relaxed more into his embrace. He wasn't judging her. A weight lifted from her shoulders. "I told you about the club and my Dom when we first discussed kink."

"You did." His arms tightened around her, and she tilted

her head up. His gaze was on her. There was concern and understanding in his face. "But why do I suspect there is more?"

"There is." She had to tell him the whole story. "I told you before about Peter's addiction. But I didn't tell you everything." She closed her eyes. "When Peter confessed he was addicted to Adderall, I gave him the name of the clinic I went to. They had a great outpatient unit, and he swore he would go and get clean."

"But he didn't."

"No. I didn't know this until the night we went to the club."

"So you mentioned."

"Yes, so when we got home, Peter apologized and went to cook a late dinner. I figured he'd finally gotten his anger out of his system, and after dinner maybe we could sit down and talk. I figured his cooking dinner was extending an olive branch."

"You don't need to go on."

"I do. I'd taken a quick shower, and when I went into the kitchen I noticed Peter's eyes were bright, and I figured it was from earlier. My stress levels were climbing. He'd poured me a glass of orange juice because he made omelets for dinner. I picked it up and took a sip." Even now she could taste the bitterness of the drugs. "All it took was one sip, and I knew what he'd done. He spiked my juice with Adderall."

"Is this man still alive?" Hassan's voice was low and tight.

"As far as I know. We fought again, and that's when he slapped me. I walked out that night and never looked back."

"Catherine knows all this?"

"Yes, we were flatmates, even though I spent a lot of time at Peter's. She helped me go back the next day and get all my things." She'd never regretted a minute of what she'd done.

"I'm glad she was there for you." He brushed a kiss over the top of her head.

"Me too."

"Is Peter the reason you haven't played until now?"

"Partially. After my Dom moved on, I wasn't comfortable with anyone else." She tilted her head back so she could see his face when she said, "And I haven't had sex either."

Shock reflected in his eyes before a smile played on his lips. "I'm privileged and honored to know I'm the first in a long time."

"I wanted you to understand about my past, and why I want to help fight the opium crisis you have here in Bashir."

"I'm honored you trust me with your story. I've never met a stronger woman."

His words made her heart swell with pride and love. Yes, she was falling in love with this man. "I think your mother might argue about that." Sara let out a laugh, all her tension leaving her.

"She might." He shifted their positions until she was lying on her back with him over her. "Right now I want to kiss you."

His lips covered hers, and Sara gave herself to the kiss. This is where she wanted to be, in Hassan's arms.

Hassan lightened his kiss and looked down into Sara's green eyes. This woman was so brave to tell him of what happened to her, but not only that, he was proud she was willing to work with him.

"I want to make love to you," he whispered against her lips.

"Please."

The word had his cock hardening. Sitting up, he stripped her nightshirt off, then stripped his own clothes off. Her tongue darted out and wet her lips, and he fought his urge to ravish her.

Instead he leaned over and brushed a light kiss over her lips before he nibbled his way down her neck to her breasts. He closed his mouth over one stiff nipple, caressing it with his tongue, making it grow even harder.

Sara's fingers tangled in his hair, holding him close. He switched to her other breast, giving it the same attention. He glanced at her face, their gazes meeting briefly before he began kissing his way to her pussy.

He shifted his body. He pushed her legs apart, and he knelt between them. "You are so beautiful."

"Hassan," she called out his name when he leaned down and swept his tongue over her slit.

"You taste of desire," he commented before he began to feast on her.

Sara couldn't keep still. Her hands clawed at the sheets on the bed as Hassan licked and tormented her. It had been too long; her stomach tightened as his tongue flicked over her clit.

"I want you so much." His words were soft. He raised himself up over her.

Sharp, relentless desire hit low in her stomach. "Then take me." She let out a cry when he moved away, but he returned a moment later with a condom between his fingers. He tore it open and slid it over his raging cock.

Hassan lowered his chest to hers. His chest hair teased her already sensitive nipples. "Ready?"

"Yes, I need you." She placed her palms on his shoulders as his dick brushed her entrance.

"I want to be gentle."

"You don't have to be. I won't break."

"No, you won't." His lips captured hers as he plunged into her.

Her cries of pleasure were muffled by his mouth. Their tongues dueled with each other while she adjusted to his hardness.

He drew back and pushed back in. "All right?"

"Never better." Emotions swirled through her body. Joy, happiness, and desire. She wanted more.

Hassan grinned at her. "Let's see if I can make it even better." He slid out and back in. Her pussy tightened around him, and she shivered with pleasure. Exquisite pleasure.

Sara lifted her legs and wrapped them around his thighs. Her back arched. He was able to get more depth. Her body began to tremble.

Their mouths met once again, and her arms tightened around his neck. Her hips met his every thrust. Tension built in her core and spread. It wasn't going to take much to push her over now.

Hassan broke the kiss, his rough breath against her cheek. "So tight, so beautiful, so mine."

"Yes," she acknowledged his claim, because she was his. Heat coiled deep within her pussy and started spreading. Her legs tightened. He shifted, and his cock touched her in the perfect spot.

Sara cried out as her climax overtook her. Red, hot tendrils of pleasure flowed through her veins, wrapping her in a sensual haze. Hassan thrust several more times before he let out a moan and went still. His cock twitched inside her. She parted her lips, trying to drag air into her lungs.

He lifted himself off her and rolled off the bed. Sara turned on her side and watched him walk into the bathroom, dispose of the condom, and then come back to bed. He drew her into his arms. His heart beat against her ear.

"You are perfect."

"No, I'm not," she said. Her eyes grew heavy. She had her faults, but for tonight she'd let them go and enjoy her time in his arms.

Hassan woke early the next morning. He gazed down at Sara's face and his heart turned over in his chest. Her confession of last night filtered through his brain. She'd tried to play down her strength, but he was familiar with how hard it was to beat an addiction.

He was careful not to jostle Sara since they'd been up so late talking and then making love. Her face was serene in slumber. She didn't realize how strong she was to overcome her addiction, to even realize she had a problem to begin with.

This was one of the reason the rehab unit was important to him, because so many of the older people had problems, but with education and support they could overcome them. Sara was a shining example of that.

He slipped his robe on and he wondered if his brother Khalid knew of Sara's addiction. Probably so. Khalid had done extensive background checks on anyone coming to visit the royal family. Hassan hadn't bothered to ask him for the file, because from the moment he'd seen Sara he was enthralled and enraptured. Plus he'd figured she'd tell him about her life when she was ready.

Her willingness to trust him made his heart swell. A part of him reminded him he needed to tell her about his past as well. He shook his head. His past wasn't something he was proud of, but then again, he and Sara had been betrayed by people they loved.

At least in his case he'd had his entire family for support. He was happy Sara had her mentor and then later Catherine for support. He'd have to thank Catherine the next time he saw her for being a good friend.

A faint knock reached his ears. He walked out of the bedroom and to the door. He undid the lock and pulled the door open a crack. Khalid stood there.

"Sorry to bother you, Hassan."

"It's okay. Sara is still asleep," he said quietly, and realized she'd never explained why she locked her doors. "What can I do for you?"

"We need to discuss your trip to the clinics."

Hassan nodded and stepped out the door, shutting it quietly behind him. He glanced down the hall and motioned to Najah. Once Najah was standing at Sara's door, he walked to his room with Khalid following.

Two days later, Sara and Hassan were in the third SUV on their way to one of the outer villages. There were six vehicles in all. Each SUV had a specialized, trained driver. In the front of each was another guard.

Najah sat in the passenger seat of their SUV. Sara smiled at him when he glanced at her. Since she and Hassan had made love two nights ago, it had been a whirlwind of activity. Sara had recruited another doctor and nurse to go with them while Hassan gathered all the supplies.

"Do you really think we need ten guards?" she asked Hassan.

"I think it's a little too much, but I was outvoted by Malik and Khalid."

Sara shrugged. "Is it that dangerous?"

"No fears, Lady Sara," Najah said. "We will all be safe."

"Not worried, Najah, I just don't want to scare the villagers with all these men." She glanced out the window. They'd left before the sun rose and stopped about an hour ago to eat breakfast on the road. It was almost midmorning, and the landscape was starting to change.

When they'd left the city proper, the trees had become sparse, but there had been lots of flowers and cacti. Occasionally she'd catch a glimpse of an animal. But now, there were more trees. Some looked like fruit trees.

She was excited to meet the villagers and to help. Their vehicles stopped near what looked like an abandon building. Hassan let out a sigh.

"Well, this tells me a lot," he said, shaking his head before he opened the door and stepped out. Sara followed suit, as the other doctor and nurse approached.

Dr. Darbi was a general practitioner at the hospital, and Aisha was one of the newer nurses. Sara had liked both of them immediately. Their security force went into the building and then came out before Najah nodded.

Hassan took Sara's hand, and they entered the building. Sara now understood why Hassan had shaken his head. This was supposed to be the new outreach clinic, but instead, the table and chairs were covered with dust and dirt.

"It wasn't like this six months ago," Dr. Darbi said.

"Good thing we brought cleaning supplies and other things," Aisha said.

Hassan's face was grim, and Sara squeezed his hand. "One step at a time, remember," she told him. While they'd prepared for the trip, Hassan had been beating himself up about what happened at the Bashir City clinic. Sara each time quietly reminded him he couldn't do everything.

He nodded as the security team brought in the cleaning supplies and set them down. Sara spied several children peeking through the grimy windows. She smiled and waved, and they giggled and ducked away.

"We have an audience," she said quietly.

"They've been outside since we stepped in here," Hassan said with a grin.

"Okay, let get to work, people." Within an hour, the clinic was taking shape. Sara finished wiping down the window to see not only children but adults milling about. "Hassan." She motioned him over to her. "Look outside."

"Let's go out and greet them." He took her hand and led her outside.

Najah and two other guards stood outside the doors, which explained why no one had dared venture inside. Sara looked up in amazement at the number of people outside. "Where did they all come from?" she asked Hassan quietly.

"The village is quite large, we're on the outskirts," he told her. "Hello, everyone."

"Prince Hassan, it is an honor to have you visit our village," an older man said, stepping forward and giving a bow.

"Please." Hassan held his hand up. "No formalities. The guards are for security, there is another doctor and nurse inside, and this is Sara." He raised their joined hands.

"Hello," Sara said, scanning the crowd. There were the old and the very young, but there was an age group missing.

"Are you going to reopen the clinic?" an older woman asked.

"I would like to," Hassan said. "Dr. Darbi and Nurse Aisha are here to help anyone who needs it. Dr. Darbi was here six months ago."

"Not you, Prince Hassan?" a younger boy asked.

"Only if necessary. I'm here to talk with everyone. I have been remiss in not coming out to the villages more often."

Sara squeezed his hand. He took too much upon himself. He was a sensitive but determined man. A man she loved.

Shock vibrated though her body. She was completely and totally in love with Hassan. What a time for her to discover it. In front of dozens of people, in a remote village, and when they couldn't be alone.

Hassan released her hand. "Come, my security team has set up a tent with tables and chairs, so we can talk." He gestured to the large white tent and began walking.

Sara started to follow when the cry of a baby caught her attention. Her gaze was drawn to a young woman standing on the edges of the crowd; she barely looked out of her teens. She rocked the child, trying to soothe it. Sara turned and walked to the woman.

"Hello, I'm Sara." The young woman's brown eyes were full of worry, and there were lines of tiredness on her face.

"I'm Naila," the young woman said.

"And this is?" Fear crossed the young woman's face at Sara's question.

"My son, Aziz." The young girl swallowed.

"Handsome young man. How old is he?" Sara kept a smile on her face, hoping to ease the young girl's fears.

"Six months." The baby continued to cry, and the young woman's eyes filled with tears.

"May I?" Sara gestured she wanted to hold the baby.

Naila's eyes widened.

"I won't take him anywhere."

Nalia nodded, and Sara took the small bundle from her. "Oh, my, Aziz, you have a mighty pair of lungs." Sara cradled the baby over her shoulder, rocking him and patting his back.

"He is usually a good baby, but the last few days he cries almost all the time," Naila said. "I am a bad mother."

"No, you are not." Sara frowned. Had no one helped this poor young girl? "Babies can't tell us what is wrong, so they cry." Just then Aziz belched, and Sara smiled. He'd stopped crying. "I suspect the poor guy has a tummy ache." There could be more, but she wouldn't say anything until she had a chance to check him over.

"Lady Sara," Najah said, approaching the pair. Naila shrank back. Okay, another clue.

"Najah, this is Naila and her son Aziz. Nalia, Najah is one of the prince's guards. He won't hurt you."

Najah nodded at Nalia. A grin split his face when he saw the little boy Sara now cradled in her arms. "Please, my lady, Naila. We've set up chairs and tables under the shelter, come sit down out of the sun."

Up until that moment, Sara hadn't noticed the sun. "Let's go sit and talk about Aziz, Nalia. I'd love to talk to you about him."

Naila nodded, but gave Najah a wide berth. Over the next hour, Sara talked with Naila. After his burp, Aziz snoozed in Sara's arms. The baby seemed pretty healthy, though a little underweight. As Naila talked, Sara was glad that her training as a nurse allowed her to keep her features neutral.

Naila talked to her about the village, but nothing personal. Things here were much worse than any of them had realized. Aziz woke suddenly and started crying.

"He is hungry," Naila said.

"Do you need to nurse him? I can find you a private area."

Naila shook her head. "My milk didn't come in."

Sara frowned. While it wasn't unheard of, she suspected it was a point of shame for Naila. She glanced around and then saw Ryan, one of the new security personnel. "Ryan."

"Yes, ma'am," Ryan said, approaching the pair.

"Would you please go ask Aisha for a bottle of the formula we brought with us?" Sara was so glad Aisha had suggested they pack some baby formula into the coolers.

"Yes, ma'am." Ryan walked away and to the clinic. It was doing a brisk business.

Sara looked over at Hassan. He was seated at a table talking with one of the older men. He'd told her on the drive out he was going to sit and talk with the villagers, to see what their issues were and where they needed help.

A few minutes later, Ryan approached with a bottle in his hand and handed it to Sara. "Thank you, Ryan." He nodded and stood off to the side. "Naila, do you want to feed him?"

Naila tilted her head. "What is that?" She pointed to the bottle.

"Baby bottle and formula." Something clicked in Sara's mind. "How have you been feeding Aziz?"

"I have a feeding cloth."

Sara frowned. "Now you can use this." Sara wiggled the bottle. "First you test it on the inside of your wrist." She showed Naila and then handed her the bottle. "If it's too hot for your skin, then it's too hot for the baby."

Naila nodded and followed Sara's instructions. "It is warm but not hot." Her eyes were wide with amazement.

"Good." Sara transferred Aziz into his mother's arms. Aziz fussed but didn't cry. "Now, slip the nipple into his mouth." Naila stared at her. "The nipple of the bottle." Sara indicated with her finger.

The young woman lowered the bottle, and Aziz's mouth opened. He started sucking before the nipple was fully settled into his mouth. Naila's eyes grew even wider.

"Why hasn't someone helped you with the baby?" While Sara had learned a lot from the young woman, she hadn't found out why none of the women helped her with her child.

"I am ashamed." Naila ducked her head.

"About what?" Sara stared at the young woman's downcast head.

"I had a baby out of wedlock."

Okay, some of the villagers were mired in the old ways, but not to help this young woman when she obviously needed it? That didn't sit well with Sara, especially since Naila had told her she was just nineteen. "They won't help you because of that? What about the baby's father?"

Naila's head rose. Her cheeks turned red, and her lips pressed together. "They think it is a sin to have a baby out of wedlock, and ... " Naila's eyes filled with tears. "I'm considered unclean because I was raped."

Outrage flowed through Sara's body. How dare these people do this to Naila and her baby? Old-fashioned was one thing, but this, in her book, bordered on the criminal. "This was not your fault, Naila."

"I was foolish, so I was. But I love my Aziz." She cradled the baby close.

"Tell me how you were foolish." Sara helped Naila pull the now-empty bottle from Aziz's mouth. She lifted the baby to her shoulder, and Sara took the bottle and set it on the small table next to her.

"My baby sister was sick one night. The clinic had the medicine, so I left the house to get it for her." A tear slipped down her cheek. "When I got to the clinic there were men there, lots of men. I was afraid, but my sister needed the medicine."

Sara nodded, a picture forming in her mind. "You were helping your sister."

"I went into the clinic. All those men, I was so afraid. But the old doctor was kind. He gave me the medicine and sent me out the back door." Aziz let out a big burp, and they both smiled.

"What happened after you left the clinic?" Sara asked softly. She suspected Naila had never spoken to anyone about this until now.

"I ran home, gave my sister the medicine, and sat with her until she went to sleep. Then I went to my bed. A noise woke me a little while later, it was dark, but there was a man leaning over my bed. He put his hand over my mouth and told me if I wanted my sister to stay alive to keep silent." Tears flowed down Naila's face.

Sara slid her chair closer to Naila's and put her arm around the girl's shoulders, giving her as much comfort as possible.

"He tore my clothes off and raped me. When he was done he told me if I ever spoke of what happened to the villagers, he'd come back, kill my baby sister, and give me to his friends."

"Where are your parents?" Sara wiped Naila's tears away with her fingers.

"Dead." Her voice was quiet.

"Where is your baby sister?" Fear for the little girl filled Sara's body.

"The villagers took her away when they realized I was pregnant. I haven't seen her in nine months."

Sara's blood boiled. First, they didn't help protect this young woman, then they shunned her for something she had no control over, and then they took away her sister. "What is her name?" Her temper flared, but she kept her tone calm.

"Tala."

"It's going to be okay. Don't leave. Stay sitting right there, because you have nothing to be ashamed of or to be blamed for. I need to do something." Sara glanced up to see Najah had replaced Ryan. She motioned to him.

"My lady."

"Please stay with Naila and make sure no one bothers her." Sara stood up.

"My lady, you cannot wander around alone."

"I'm going over to see Hassan."

Najah nodded, then smiled at Naila, who ducked her head.

Sara fought not to glare at the villagers who were staring at Naila. Sara waited until Hassan was done talking with an older gentleman before she approached him.

"I didn't realize how bad things were," Hassan commented, standing up and stretching.

"I don't think anyone did. I need your help."

"What can I do for you?"

Sara quickly outlined what she had found out from and about Naila, the village, and her baby sister. By the time she was done, Hassan was frowning and his hands were clenched at his sides.

"This is unacceptable." He ran his hand over his face. "We are more modern than this atrocity."

"I know." She placed her hand on his tense forearm. "But have you noticed? Only the very young or the very old are here today. No men or women in their twenties or thirties."

Hassan glanced at the villagers milling around. "How did I not notice?"

"You are concentrating on building back relationships, and that's fine. But we need to find out where these men and women are. I have my suspicions."

Hassan's eyebrows raised. "Tell me."

"I'm guessing, but based on what Naila told me, I think Kalif's men have taken them to work in the poppy fields."

"But no one has said anything."

"I know." She tightened her hold on his arm. "Have you noticed how the older men can't seem to stand still? The dilation of their pupils? The women look around as if they expect something to happen?"

"I noticed, but ... " Hassan let out a groan. "I didn't make the connection."

"It needs to be addressed, but I don't think the security we have is going to be enough if Kalif's men come to the village."

"No worries." Hassan motioned to Ryan.

"Yes, sir."

"Ryan, I need the sat phone."

Ryan handed Hassan a big black phone. Hassan punched

a button and then put it to his ear. "Khalid, it's way worse than we thought. How soon can you get here with a full security contingency?" He listened and nodded. "Good. I'll let everyone know, and we'll move the villagers out of the line of fire." Hassan handed the phone back to Ryan. "Scope out somewhere we can safely assemble the villagers. Do it quietly."

Ryan nodded and left. Sara glanced up at Hassan. "What are you planning?"

"Kalif is always one step ahead of us. By our coming out here unannounced, we are able to see exactly what is going on. As long as no one reports to Kalif, we have a chance."

"To do what?"

"Raid the poppy farm."

Sara tensed. "The villagers will be at risk."

"Which is why we need someplace safe for them, and us as well." He snagged her around the waist and rested his forehead against hers. "You stay close to Naila and her baby. You are probably the only one she trusts. Najah will stay with you."

"Hassan." Fear crowded into her mind.

"I want you safe."

"What about you?"

"I'll be safe. I promise." He lifted his head as Ryan approached.

"Sir, there are several large abandoned buildings about two blocks over. We can use them," Ryan said.

"Inform the rest of the security team. I'm going to start sending villagers in that direction." Ryan nodded and left. Hassan turned back to her, his blue eyes dull. "Go. Take Naila and her baby with you, and don't leave Najah's side."

"Be safe, my love." She brushed her lips over his before leaving his embrace. She said a silent prayer before she made her way back to Naila that everything would go well.

Hassan urged the villagers toward the empty buildings. Many were reluctant to go, but he would smile, telling them it was for their safety and that of their families. It was slow going, but it was working.

"Please, Prince Hassan, help me." A young girl ran up to him, her hands tugging at his pants, tears running down her cheeks.

"Forgive my daughter," a man said, walking up to them. "My daughter isn't herself today."

"I am not your daughter." The young girl stared up at the man, defiance in her brown eyes.

The man opened his mouth, but Hassan held up his hand for silence. He'd seen this man on the outskirts of the men he'd talked to earlier. Hassan knelt down and placed his hands on the young girl's shoulders. "What is your name?"

"Tala." Her voice was quiet while she wiped her cheeks.

"He's not my father, my real father is dead, and they took me from my sister."

"Your sister is unclean," the man spat out.

Hassan glared at the man as understanding hit him. He was positive this was Naila's little sister. At least she'd been found without having to question the entire village. "Everything will be okay, Tala. Trust me."

The girl nodded. Hassan stood and took her hand in his. She trembled in his hold, and his anger renewed. He turned his attention to the man claiming to be her father. There were no signs of opium addiction, but that didn't mean anything. "Follow me," he said.

"But, Prince Hassan," the man started to protest.

"I'm taking Tala to a safe place, it's up to you if you follow or not." Hassan started walking with Tala at his side. He didn't look back to see if the man followed or not. Once they reached the buildings, he quietly asked one of his guards to go find Sara.

He knelt down in front of Tala. "When Sara gets here, please go with her. She will keep you safe."

"Will you find my sister and keep her safe?"

"Yes, little one. I have a feeling she is already here and safe." He glanced up as Sara approached. There were lines of worry around her forehead. "Sweetheart?" He stood and brushed his fingers over her cheek.

"It's okay. I'm dealing." She smiled, but it didn't reach her eyes. She glanced at the young girl next to him.

"Sara, this is Tala. Tala, this is Sara, she will take good care of you."

"Oh, Hassan." Sara's eyes filled with tears. "Thank you." She kissed his cheek.

"Keep her with you and Naila," Hassan said in her ear. "Advise Najah, no one is to separate you from them." He wasn't going to take any chances. Najah would defend the women with his life if needed. Hassan hoped it wouldn't come to that.

"Tala." He knelt down so his face was level with the young girl. "This is my girlfriend, Sara. Go with her, and she'll keep you safe. I promise you'll see your sister soon."

A huge smile lit up Tala's face. He stood. Then Tala placed her hand into Sara's. Hassan cupped Sara's chin and gave her a quick hard kiss. "To keep me going," he commented before walking away.

Sara touched her lips and then smiled. "Let's go, Tala." She led the young girl through the room. The villagers began whispering, but none stopped her. Maybe because earlier when they started making comments about Naila, Sara had told them to stop being rude, and then Najah stepped forward, telling them he was ashamed of his own people. Since then they'd given her a wide birth.

Tala let out a cry when she saw Naila sitting on the floor with the baby on her lap. "Naila." The girl tugged her hand from Sara's and ran to her sister.

A tear made its way down Sara's cheek, and she brushed it away.

"This is a good thing you do," a woman said from behind Sara.

She turned to see one of the village women standing there, her hands clasped together in front of her. "Thank you."

"The old ways are old. We must learn new ways. Our children deserve it."

Sara took a deep breath. Progress. "I'm glad to hear you feel that way." She glanced over at Tala when she heard a giggle.

"Go, be with them. I will talk with the others. It's time for us to be the people of Bashir once again. To be proud." The woman walked away, and Sara shook her head. Maybe this would all work out after all.

She joined Naila and Tala. She would talk to Hassan later about taking them back to Bashir City with them.

Thirty minutes later, Hassan stood at the edge of the village as Khalid and the security force arrived. They'd finally finished getting the last of the villagers inside the buildings.

"Everyone inside?" Khalid asked.

"Yes." Hassan glanced at his brother. He and his men

were dressed in black, their faces and heads covered by black headdresses.

"I'm hoping this won't take long. But no matter what you hear, do not leave here. Ryan," Khalid called.

"Yes, sir."

"Stay with Hassan and keep him here and safe."

"Yes, boss."

Hassan glared at his brother. It was bad enough Khalid was in harm's way.

"Don't give me that look. Mom would never forgive me if something happened to you," Khalid said.

"And how do you think she'd feel if something happened to you?"

"Good point. I will be careful." The brothers grasped forearms before Khalid and the security force strode away. They would make their way to the poppy fields on foot. Hassan paced while he waited. He would stay out here and defend the villagers and Sara if it became necessary. After an hour he could hear the villagers getting restless, but they would all just have to wait.

"They're back," Ryan said thirty minutes later. Hassan stopped his pacing to see his brother, the security force, and a group of men and women walking toward the buildings.

"Inside the building you will find your families," Khalid said to the men and women. The second they entered the building cries went up.

"How bad?" Hassan asked.

"No one hurt on our side. Their side is another matter." Khalid tilted his head and moved away from the building. Hassan followed. "It's worse than we thought. The men and women of the village are being used as slave labor, told if they don't cooperate their families will be killed."

Hassan closed his eyes. "The women … are they unharmed?"

"From what I could ascertain, the men were told to leave the women alone."

Hassan sighed. That was good news. "What do we do?"

"I suggest moving the entire village closer to the city." Khalid held up his hand when Hassan opened his mouth. "Twofold, brother. One, Kalif can't force them back to the fields, and two, if he retaliates the village is empty."

"Agreed, but how are we going to do this?" Hassan drew his hand through his hair. Moving the village wasn't going to be easy.

"Way ahead of you. I called Malik. He's sending out buses as we speak. They're old school buses, but they'll work. After interrogating some of Kalif's men, I've discovered his main base is about a day's travel from here, so it will be a while before he can get here."

"Now I have to convince the villagers to leave."

"Somehow I don't think that will be a problem." Khalid walked away when one of the security men called his name.

Hassan moved into the building. Conversations and crying overwhelmed him. He moved through the room, finally spotting Sara with Naila and Tala. Sara noticed him first. She ran to him and threw herself into his arms.

"I'm fine." He hugged her to him. "I was right outside the building the entire time."

"Khalid?" She leaned back to look at him.

"Fine. No losses on our side." He glanced over her shoulder at Naila and Tala. "We're taking you back to Bashir City with us." Tala's eyes grew wide and Naila's mouth fell open. "I want you to tell Najah where your home is and what you need from it."

"There's not much." Naila said ducking her head. "Go straight down the street to our left, I'm the last hut on the right." Naila pointed which direction to go. "I just need a few things for the baby."

Najah nodded. "I will get your things." He turned and left.

"You really mean it? We're going with you?" Tala asked, excitement in her voice.

"Yes. The whole village is." He turned and clapped his hands. The room quieted. "Everyone, as you can see by the return of your loved ones, the poppy field has been raided. Transportation is on its way to move everyone closer to Bashir City."

"Abandon our homes?" a male voice called out, and others began talking.

Hassan raised his hand, and silence fell again. "I understand this may be difficult, but many of you have expressed concerns about retaliation. I'm not going to force anyone to leave, it is your choice." He glanced around the room, making sure to meet the gazes of the elders of the village. "Think about your children. They will be taken again to work the fields." A slight murmur went up from the group. "Transportation will be here within two hours. If you want to leave, go home and pack your personal belongings, and meet back here."

Voices rose as the people filed out of the building. Khalid strode in. Hassan and his brother made their way over to the ladies.

"Do you think they'll come?" Sara asked.

"I hope so, because we're burning the poppy field as soon as they're on their way," Khalid said.

"How long will you be after we've left?" Hassan asked. It was getting late; it would be dark before they made it back to Bashir City.

"Not more than an hour. We're taking our vehicles so we can get out once we set it ablaze," Khalid said.

Hassan nodded. Khalid turned to leave, but Sara put her hand on his arm. "Please be careful, Khalid." She went up on her toes and kissed his cheek. Hassan was amazed to see his brother's cheek darken. "I will," Khalid said. Then he left.

Sara moved to his side, and he put his arm around her waist. "He'll be safe," Hassan said.

"He better be, or your mother will have his butt."

Hassan laughed. "You are so good for me."

Sara settled Naila, Tala, and Aziz into one of the SUVs. She refused to let them ride on the buses with the villagers. They'd abused Naila and her family more than enough.

"Now if you need anything, Nigel will take care of you." She pointed to the man sitting in the passenger seat. "He'll make sure you stay safe as we drive to Bashir City."

"I promise to radio if there's an issue, Lady Sara."

Sara smiled. Most of the security staff had taken to calling her that. She shut the door and made her way to the SUV in front of this one where Hassan waited for her. The buses were loaded and ready to go.

All but a handful of villagers had decided to join them. Khalid decided it was better for them to go as one big caravan than to separate. He'd taken minimal forces to burn the poppy field, leaving the rest of the security force to escort them home.

Hassan motioned for her to climb inside the vehicle, then followed her. Within a few minutes they were on their way. Sara let out a sigh.

"Tired?" Hassan asked.

"A little bit."

Hassan unfastened his safety belt, slid to the middle seat, and refastened the belt. He put his arm around her shoulder and pulled her to him. "Why don't you try to rest?"

"I'm not sure I can." She laid her hand on his shoulder. It

had been a long day, and it wasn't over yet. "Where are we going to put everyone?"

"We have a set of apartments on the outskirts of the city that were finished a few months ago. Rafi took charge when Malik suggested bringing the villagers to town. They're being cleaned, and he's making sure everything is in order as we drive."

"Your family works miracles." Sara yawned and her lashes drifted shut.

"You're the miracle worker, my Sara," Hassan whispered.

Hassan finally relaxed a few days later. They had all been busy getting the villagers settled, but also making sure everyone was healthy and getting the older people the care they needed to get off the opium. Sara had helped Naila, Tala, and Aziz settle into one of the apartments.

Everyone, except Hassan's parents, was milling around the sitting room enjoying some quiet time. Now maybe he and Sara could have some quiet time together. They'd been running in opposite directions for the last few days, with some quick lovemaking before falling asleep. He enjoyed holding her in his arms each night.

"I can't believe we did it." Sara sat onto the sofa.

"You and Hassan did most of the work," Catherine said.

Sara shook her head. "Hassan was a rock in all this."

"I'm happy the villagers are mostly willing to accept help for their addiction. And they are mostly liking the apartments," Hassan said, taking a seat next to her. He was tired, but happy.

"It is good," Malik said. "And ... "

The sofa shook and the windows rattled before the sound of an explosion reached their ears. Everyone froze in place, then chaos descended. The guards and security staff flowed into the room.

"Earthquake?" Sara asked, her eyes wide.

Hassan shook his head, looking to where Malik was talking with Samir and Khalid. He stood when Malik frowned and Khalid swore. Sara stood as well, taking his hand.

"What happened?" Catherine asked, her face pale.

"Someone set off an explosion near the marketplace," Khalid said.

"How many hurt?" Hassan asked.

"Unknown." Khalid looked at his men, and they shook their heads.

"I need to get out there," Hassan said, his mind running through the possible scenarios. Sara grabbed his arm.

"Not yet," Malik said. "Khalid has sent security forces out to check for any other bombs."

"People could be dying," he protested.

"Hassan," Rafi said, "the explosions are on the edge and luckily at this hour most of the stores were closed."

"I'm a doctor."

"And I'm a nurse. We don't know the full situation. Please wait," Sara said quietly. "Wait until they have a chance to make sure there are no other explosions. You can't help people if something happens to you." Her voice broke off.

The sheen of tears in Sara's eyes had him pulling her into his arms. She was correct, but he didn't have to like it. "Only for you."

The next thirty minutes the tension in the room grew and grew, until Khalid reported there didn't seem to be any more bombs. He also reported that the damage was minimal.

"I still need to go out and check on our people," Hassan said.

"And I'm going with you," Sara said.

"No, too dangerous." He wasn't about to let her put herself in danger.

"You'll need help," she said. Hassan opened his mouth, but Sara glared at him. "Don't go all alpha male on me. I'm a nurse, and I can help. The longer we argue, the less help we can be."

Hassan sighed. "All right, but Najah stays by your side."

"No problem," she said.

Sara climbed out of the SUV with Najah at her side. The smell of dust, dirt, and gunpowder assaulted her nose. The eerie quietness made her shiver. While it was still light, it was after six in the evening.

"Khalid is right, this part of town was pretty much empty," Hassan said, pulling out backpacks with big red crosses on them.

"That's a good thing." Sara took one of the backpacks and slipped it on, while Hassan, Najah, and two other body-guards did the same.

"Be alert." Hassan ran his fingers over her cheek. "I don't like the thought of you being in danger."

"I feel the same about you." She rubbed her cheek into his palm, then turned her head and kissed the center of it.

His blue eyes flared with concern. "Just be careful." He took her hand, and they began to walk. There were a few people out on the street. They treated minor scratches and scrapes.

While Hassan talked with a group of people, she slowly made her way down the street. Najah was conversing with the other bodyguards. She treated a few people, but all and all it looked like they'd been pretty lucky.

She turned a corner to see Tala running toward her. "Tala." She knelt down as the little girl flew into her arms.

"Lady Sara, bad man came. He's scary."

Sara stiffened. "What bad man?"

"I don't know. Big boom and then he was there. Naila pushed me out the window and told me to run. I'm so glad to find you." The little girl was trembling.

Naila was in trouble. Sara stood. The apartment building was not far away. "Tala, go around the corner, Najah is there, tell him what is going on. I'll go help Naila." She pushed Tala toward the corner and then took off at a jog toward the apartments.

Hassan would be furious with her, but she wasn't going to wait for anyone. Naila was in trouble, and she was going to help her. When she got to the building, she shed the backpack and set it out of the way, then crept into the hallway and down to Naila's apartment.

The door was cracked open. Sara peeked inside. There was a man dressed head to toe in black, and he was speaking rapidly in Arabic. While Sara had begun to have a good grasp of the language, he was speaking a little too fast for her to catch more than a word or two. And what she heard she didn't like.

She held still as the man began circling around Naila and Aziz. Thankfully, Aziz was asleep in his mother's arms. Naila cradled the baby protectively against her body. Sara waited until the man was clear of the door and far enough away from Naila to facilitate an escape.

Sara flung the door open, grabbed Naila by the arm, and pushed her to the door. "Run to Hassan," she said, pushing Naila out the door. Sara made sure Naila was clear before she started to follow.

"No, you don't." A male arm curved around her waist and flung her across the room.

Sara landed against the wall, which knocked the breath out of her. She leaned against it, fighting to get air into her lungs. "What do you want with Naila and her baby?" she asked. Thank goodness Naila had run.

"I don't want Naila, but I want my son."

"Your son." The man's face was still covered, so she couldn't get a good look at him, but anger filled her. "How dare you?" She didn't even think about what words were coming out of her mouth. "You rape her and then expect her to allow you to take *her* son?"

"Shut up."

"I will not." Sara let her voice grow louder. If she kept the man distracted, maybe someone would hear her voice.

"I said shut up, bitch." He slapped her across the face.

Bells rang in her head as it snapped to one side. Pain almost made her knees buckle, but she didn't bother to reach for her cheek. There would be a bruise there tomorrow, but she could handle it.

"I don't have time for this." He pulled something from his pocket, and Sara recognized the pipe for smoking opium.

"What is your name?" she asked, trying to keep calm and slow her breathing down.

"Osman, not that it matters." He lit the pipe and took a deep draw before letting it out. Smoke filled the air. "You'll be dead before anyone can rescue you."

Fear invaded her veins, but she fought to keep calm. Hassan would be here. Tala and Naila should have reached him by now. More smoke filled the room, and Sara put her hand over her nose and mouth.

"You don't like." An evil glint flashed in his eyes. Before she knew it, he moved, grabbed her arm, and pulled it behind her back. Her chest hit his. "I will make you like." He took a pull on the pipe.

Sara turned her head away and held her breath. Osman twisted her arm. She opened her mouth in a gasp, and he blew the smoke right into her face. She coughed, and he did it again.

She fought to keep her breath in short bursts to keep the drugs out of her system. She used her free hand to knock the pipe from him, and it crashed to the floor. "Wild woman." He tangled his fingers in her hair. "Maybe I keep you for my men. They would love a wild woman to warm their bed."

"Not in this lifetime." Sara struggled with Osman even as the opium penetrated her system. She wouldn't give up without a fight. Where was Hassan? He should be here by now.

Had something happened to Tala and Naila? Tears filled her eyes when Osman pulled her head back using her hair.

"Maybe I'll take a sample."

Her muscles were starting to grow lax. Once that happened, he could do anything he wanted to her. No fucking way. Sara shifted carefully, brought her knee up, and hit him in the groin. Osman cried out.

But he held her so close, it only stunned him. He still

retained his hold on her. "I should kill you for that, but my men will make you wish you were dead." He spun her around and marched her toward the door.

She had barely cleared the doorway when Osman cried out. The hold on her hair was released, and she was pulled away into another set of male arms. "Hassan," she whispered as she was crushed against his body.

"Sara, sweetheart." His voice was soft.

"Need oxygen." She had to get the drugs out of her system.

Hassan's stomach was in his throat. Tala had run to him telling him what had happened. He, Najah, Ryan, and Khalid had started running when they ran into Naila. He had Ryan take her and Aziz to Tala and asked him to wait with them.

When they saw Sara being pushed out the door, Khalid and Najah took defensive positions on either side of the door. The second they hit the man, Hassan pulled her to him.

"I've got it," Khalid said, opening the backpack Sara had left in the hallway.

Hassan was so glad he'd added small oxygen bottles to the packs. They wouldn't last long, but they would help. Khalid handed it to him, and he turned it on before holding the mask up to Sara's face.

The sweet perfume smell of opium lingered in the hall. She took several deep breaths, then pushed his hand away. "He blew opium smoke in my face. He was trying to take Aziz." Her words came out in a rush.

He put the oxygen mask back over her face. Already he could see her eyes clearing up. Hassan glanced over to where Khalid and Najah stood. The man had his hands tied behind his back. "Unwrap his head scarf."

Najah did as asked.

"Osman?" Hassan couldn't believe it. What was his dead ex-fiancée Fatima's brother doing here?

"Hello, Hassan. Had I known she was yours, I would have taken her away first instead of playing with her."

"You know him?" Sara asked.

"Yes." Hassan glared at the man he had once called a friend. "Why did you try to take Aziz?"

"Because he's my son."

Before Hassan could say a word, Najah drew back his fist and punched Osman. Osman fell to the floor. Without a word, Najah picked him up.

"You deserved that," Najah said to Osman, then looked at Hassan, who nodded.

"Why are you working for Kalif?" He was taking a guess, but based on what they'd briefly heard, he had his suspicions.

"Why not?" Osman gave a bitter laugh. "After you killed Fatima, what did I have to live for?"

Sara stiffened in his arms. Hassan looked down at her. Her eyes were normal now, and she was standing on her own. He shook his head and returned his gaze to Osman. This wasn't the way he wanted her to hear about his past.

"I didn't kill Fatima, she did that to herself. Or should I say the drugs did?"

Sara pulled his hand away from where he was holding the oxygen to her face. "I'm okay. He's under the influence still."

"I know, sweetheart." He tightened his arm around her waist, keeping her close to him.

"He needs help."

"He'll get it." The rehab unit was up and running. No matter how much he might want to throw Osman in jail, he'd get the help he needed first.

"You helped her get the drugs," Osman yelled. "You were supposed to protect her, to keep her safe. She was going to be your wife."

"Wife?" Sara's voice was soft.

"Enough." Hassan's anger cut through the air. "Khalid, take him to the rehab unit. Put a twenty-four-hour guard on him. We'll keep him in seclusion until he's fully detoxed, then we'll find out what he knows."

"Good enough." Khalid grabbed Osman, and they walked away, Osman protesting the entire time.

"I think we need to talk," Sara said.

Hassan nodded. It wasn't a talk he was looking forward to. They exited the building to see Tala, Naila, who was holding Aziz, and Ryan walking their way.

"Lady Sara," Tala cried, running up to her. Sara bent down and scooped up the little girl.

"You did good, Tala."

"I ran like you told me, then when Naila came and told me you got her out, and the prince was on his way to save you, I knew everything would be fine, and I was right." The words rushed out of the little girl's mouth.

"We're all safe." Sara glanced up at Naila.

"Osman?" Naila asked.

"You're safe. He won't bother you again," Hassan said, his voice gentle. "Why don't we go back to the cars? Naila, you, Tala, and Aziz will spend the night at the palace with us. Your apartment needs to be aired out."

"The palace." There was awe in Tala's voice.

"Yes, the palace." Hassan scooped the little girl up into his arms. He held her on his left side, while his right arm secured Sara to his side. He wouldn't take a chance of losing her again.

A couple hours later, Sara was almost asleep on her feet. When they got back to the palace, she saw to Tala and Naila getting settled. Then Catherine started fussing over Sara when she heard what had happened.

Hassan and Khalid told Malik everything that had happened and about Osman. Sara was in her room when he arrived, telling Catherine she wanted nothing more than a hot shower and bed. Catherine gave him a pointed look before she left Sara's rooms.

He didn't say a word. He walked over to Sara, picked her up, and carried her to his room and then to his bathroom. He turned on the shower and stripped off her clothes and then his own. They stepped into the shower, and he held her close.

Sara let out a groan as the water hit her body.

"I almost lost you today."

"You came in time." Her fingers traced the frown on his forehead.

He turned her around, shampooed her hair, and then gently washed her body. By the time they were done, she could barely keep her eyes open. It didn't surprise him.

Hassan dried her off, then carried her to his bed. He cradled her against him. "I'm so sorry," he whispered.

"For what?" Her voice was sleepy.

"For everything." He glanced down at her face and saw she was asleep. Good. They could talk tomorrow. With everything that had happened in the last few days, he had a long night ahead of him. There were some decisions he had to make, because he was going to protect the woman he loved no matter what it cost him. Even if it meant Sara leaving him.

Sara woke and stretched. She winced when her muscles

protested. The events of the previous day rushed back. She sat up, surprised to find herself alone in bed.

"Are you okay?"

Sara saw Catherine sitting in one of the chairs. "Just a little sore. What are you doing here?" She was still in Hassan's bedroom.

"Hassan made me promise to be here when you woke up."

Sara's senses went on alert. "Where is he?"

Catherine shook her head. Sara just stared at her friend, then she climbed out of bed and slipped on her robe. "Tell me." Her stomach clenched. Why did she have this feeling Hassan was about to do something noble that he didn't have to do?

"He's getting ready to hold a press conference. Hassan is going to step down as the minister of health and resign from the hospital."

"Like hell." Sara stormed into the bathroom and then yelped when she saw herself in the mirror. "Well, that's one hell of bruise." Her entire cheek was multicolored.

"Hassan is determined. You haven't seen the morning papers, but he has."

"Show me." Sara wasn't about to let Hassan give up his work, his passion. It was what helped him be the man he is.

"I've got tea and scones waiting along with the papers."

Sara nodded. "Give me a few seconds to clean up." Sara brushed her teeth and hair before joining Catherine in

Hassan's sitting room. She took a seat on the sofa and picked up the first paper.

She read the first paragraph and threw it down, then picked up the second one. She didn't even make it past the first two lines before she threw it down and accepted the cup of tea Catherine held out to her. She took a sip, then looked at Catherine.

"It's nothing but speculation and lies. How long to the press conference?"

"About thirty minutes."

"All right, not much time. I need you to get Najah and Ryan while I get dressed. Here's what I'm thinking."

Thirty-two minutes later, Sara smoothed her hand down the caftan filled with the royal colors and took a deep breath. This time she was aware of what wearing it meant. She closed her eyes and thought about what she was about to do.

Catherine walked up with Tala and Naila. Hassan and his brothers were already inside the press room, along with Najah and the other security guards. "Naila, I really don't want to bring you and Tala into this," Sara said.

"We want to help," Naila said.

"All right. I'll walk in first, and you three follow." Sara took another deep breath, turned the knob, and walked into the room. All talking ceased and all eyes turned toward her, including those of the man she loved.

She hadn't told him that yet. Head held high and a slight smile on her lips, she walked to Hassan and kissed him on the cheek. A gasp went up from the room when they saw her face. She refused to hide the bruise with makeup; she wanted the world to see what had happened.

"What are you doing here?" he whispered, as she took his hand in hers and nudged him to the side.

"Not allowing you to make a mistake," she said in a low tone before turning to face the room. It was full of reporters, not unusual, but this time there were TV cameras as well.

Butterflies filled her tummy. "Good morning, everyone. I'm sorry to be late." She smiled and nodded at everyone in the room. "I know it's been a few crazy days for all of us, but I'm here because ... " She glanced up at Hassan, then over at Catherine who stood next to Malik. Catherine nodded. "Because I don't want Hassan to make a mistake. You see, Hassan was about to announce his resignation from the hospital and as the minister of health."

Voices rose, along with protests. Sara held her hand up, and they quieted. Hassan's fingers tightened around hers, and she squeezed back. She held her ground when he tried to nudge her out of the way.

"You see," she continued, "I love this man." She kept her gaze on him. "He takes on too much responsibility for things he can't control. He believes what happened to me is his fault, but it's not."

Hassan shook his head. "Sara," he started.

"No, Hassan, they need to know." Sara turned back to the group. "I know you've all seen my bruise." She gestured toward her cheek. "This was given to me by one of Kalif's men yesterday. There are some things you should know; actually, all the people of Bashir should know." She glanced over at Naila and Tala, and they took a small step forward. "This is Naila and her sister Tala. Circumstances created a hard life for them, but they never complained and did their best. Last night the man who hit me tried to take Naila's baby from her. This man was one who worked with Kalif and his opium operation."

The reporters started to mumble.

"He was also responsible for the bombs," Khalid said. "He'd hoped to use them as a distraction."

"It worked. Tala found me and told me what was going on, and I, without thinking, went alone to help." A shiver worked its way up her spine. Things could have turned out so differently. "I was able to get Naila and her baby to safety, but the man grabbed me." She touched her bruised cheek. "I didn't come out unscathed."

"Lady Sara," a reporter called out.

Sara held up her hand. "Please, if we can do questions at the end." The reporter nodded, and she was grateful. She was barely holding onto her nerve as it was. "The man began smoking opium and blowing it in my face." Her voice cracked.

Hassan disentangled their hands and put his arm around her waist, pulling her to his side. His strength gave her the courage to continue.

"I'm susceptible to opium because I was once addicted." Gasps and words of disbelief reached her ears. "I'm not proud of it, but when I realized I had a problem, with help I was able to kick the habit. When the man blew smoke in my face I started to fall under its spell, but luckily Hassan, Khalid, and Najah were able to subdue him and rescue me."

The room burst out in applause.

"But Bashir can't tolerate the poppy growing in this country. It will only continue to get worse. I ask the people of Bashir to speak up when they see something that isn't right. If you have a problem, let us help you."

"What happened to the man?" a reporter yelled.

"He's currently in the hospital's rehab unit undergoing detox protocol," Hassan said.

"Prince Hassan, why were you going to resign?" another reporter asked.

"If you remember, years ago, I was engaged. Fatima was addicted to opium, unknown to me. When I found out, I tried to help her, but she didn't want help. I broke off the engagement."

"Yes, I remember," another reporter said. "Didn't she die?"

Hassan sighed. "Fatima did. The man who hurt Sara last night was her brother." Again the voices in the room rose. "His intention was to take Sara with him and give her to his men."

"They must be stopped," a female voice yelled.

"What about Kalif? He's one of the tribal leaders," another reporter said.

"He's still at large," Malik commented. "For years the poppies have been a problem. Sara is right, things must change." Malik threw back his shoulders. "We will no longer tolerate the kidnapping and forced labor of our village children, nor will we let anyone exploit or harm our young women."

Khalid stepped forward. "I have started a special security force, you've seen them around. They are here to protect the citizens of Bashir. Hassan is going to be traveling from village to village, making sure they have the help they need. We know the poppy growing is mainly in the north, and we will concentrate our efforts there to rid ourselves of this terrible drug."

Sara had no idea so many decisions had been made. But they were the right decisions, and she would help the royal family in any way she could.

"Well done," a reporter yelled.

"There is one more thing I would like to announce," Malik said. "It was decided this morning that the new drug rehabilitation unit will be called the Fairchild Drug Rehabilitation Unit."

Sara's head whipped around, and she stared at Malik. He grinned and winked at her.

"This was decided among the staff of the hospital. If any citizen of Bashir needs help overcoming their addiction, they are welcome to come in and will be treated free of charge. In order to keep our country strong, our citizens must be strong."

"And," Rafi stepped forward, "we need to find a way to help our younger citizens. In the next month, with the help of the Crown Princess, we will be rolling out new educational reforms and apprentices programs. Free of charge to all Bashir citizens."

The room burst into applause, and Sara smiled. She'd taken a risk, and it had paid off. As the room quieted down, Sara heard a faint chanting.

Khalid strode to the balcony doors and opened them. The chanting grew louder. Khalid glanced out and then motioned them to join him.

Hassan took her hand and pulled her to the balcony. The people of Bashir filled the public courtyard, chanting for Bashir and the royal family. Sara grinned. This was wonderful. She turned to tell Hassan to see him grinning at her before he took her hand and got down on one knee.

Her breath caught in her throat. What was he doing? The chanting grew silent.

"Sara Fairchild." His voice was strong and loud. "I love you with all my heart. Will you become my wife? My princess?"

Her chest swelled, and tears filled her eyes. "I love you so much, Hassan. I would be honored to become your wife."

The reporters cheered, and one of them yelled, "She said yes! Another royal wedding."

Hassan drew her to her feet and they kissed. When they broke apart, the crowd was chanting once again, but this time her and Hassan's names.

"Are we okay?" Hassan asked softly.

"Never better, my love. I love you with all my heart."

"The same for me."

His lips captured hers, and the crowd cheered.

ABOUT THE AUTHOR

Marie Tuhart lives in the beautiful Pacific Northwest with her muse, Penny, a four-pound toy poodle. She loves to read and write. When Marie's not writing, she spends time with family, traveling and enjoying life.

Marie is a multi-published author with The Wild Rose Press, Trifecta Publishing House and does some self-publishing. You can join Marie's newsletter where she gives her group advance information on her books, runs contests, and hosts giveaways just for newsletter readers. Marie can also be found on Goodreads, Pinterest, Twitter, and Facebook.

ACKNOWLEDGMENTS

Always, to my critique group who support me.